London Fell is a widely published author of political and legal thought issues over a series of 12 books. His new found literary works are now being produced over a number of individual books. He is a graduate of Princeton University and holds a doctorate degree from Columbia University.

To Sophia, Alexander, and Jason (editor-in-chief).

London Fell

THE PAINTER'S DREAM MACHINE

THIRD NOVEL IN A TRILOGY

AUSTIN MACAULEY PUBLISHERS™

LONDON • CAMBRIDGE • NEW YORK • SHARJAH

Ordering Information
Quantity sales: Special discounts are available on quantity purchases by corporations, associations, and others. For details, contact the publisher at the address below.

Publisher's Cataloging-in-Publication data
Fell, London
The Painter's Dream Machine

ISBN 9781647507008 (Paperback)
ISBN 9781647507015 (ePub e-book)

Library of Congress Control Number: 2021920799

www.austinmacauley.com/us

First Published 2021
Austin Macauley Publishers LLC
40 Wall Street, 33rd Floor, Suite 3302
New York, NY 10005
USA

mail-usa@austinmacauley.com
+1 (646) 5125767

Table of Contents

Prefatory Note

The first and second novels in the trilogy are *Claudette Monet in America: Fantasy Sketches* and *New York Blast-Off*.

Part One

Inventing the Machine

Chapter One
Boston Rebirth: Heroes and Antiheroes

Theirs became an ever-evolving saga series that found its way eventually to Boston and vicinity (following two previous novels).

This was for them the premier American center for intellectual institutions of all kinds—literary, artistic, technological, and more. It was the most celebrated city center for colleges and universities in vast array, drawing throngs of students, visitors, and residents to its unique historical and cultural opportunities.

The Topping couple, Olivia and Oliver, living together but not married, were irresistibly drawn to all this when moving there in their later years, now freer from their earlier boundaries and preoccupations. She with her artistic interests as a painter and he with his journalistic and technological interests all seemed a natural fit for two people who had grown restless in their small-town Iowa background, and also later in New York for him and San Francisco for her.

The closely bonded, albeit unmarried pair took up residence together in a small apartment inside an old Victorian-era house along Commonwealth Avenue. This was a central grand old boulevard, lined within center mall and magnificent historic houses on either side, stretching for a number of miles from Back Bay and public gardens all the way out toward the Charles River and Newton. On or near this throughway were many of the kinds of institutions and centers already alluded to. Walking these streets and neighborhoods as the pair loved to do made them feel as if stepping back into late 19th-century places and spaces.

Not far from their house by Commonwealth Avenue lay the small liberal arts Emerald College, where they signed up as auditors for various courses suiting their interests. Olivia found the advanced artistic practice sessions much to her liking. True to form and his earlier dreamer geek reputation before growing into a prominent journalist before retiring, Oliver was fascinated by the slant given to the college's technology programs. They learned that Emerald College's very name was intended by its founders to convey a sense of the institution's liberal jewelry-like array of courses based on self-designed free-wheeling loosely structured approaches, setting the Emerald College apart from more rigidly structured places like Harvard or M.I.T. at the other end of the spectrum. By now themselves more loosely structured and open to looser outlooks on 'experimentation', that is, more laidback, the pair found ready acceptance by the much younger college-age students who filled their classes.

The Topping couple, not married but seeming to be in an unusual dynamic going back to their younger years, found a ready access into the college's student body, partly because of their love of the younger generations in which they could find substitutes for the children they themselves never had, partly also because of their friendly eagerness to learn new things. From these contacts, they learned quickly enough about which courses and teachers to take, though popularity was often an uncertain mixture of private appreciation and public perception.

"In the realm of the abnormal can sometimes be found," according to Olivia, "a pathway to the normal. Through the leading of strange occurrences can sometimes open up new dimensions with promise. So unusual an outlook as parapsychology and its psych phenomena can open up a vast new world of possibilities. Reacting off each other in a series of experiences or events, the heroes and antiheroes come together in a compelling drama. The one brings out qualities in the other into a driven dialectic. Good and evil are typically not one without the other, nor even perceptible as such, requiring one to accentuate the other."

"In any case," Oliver foresaw, "such phenomena as supersensory perception open up vast new possibilities for heroes and antiheroes acting in concert with the painter's eye and dream machine. Of course, advanced social media, smartphones, super computers, and telepathy can be accessed by both heroes and antiheroes for good or evil. Which would it be?"

Chapter Two

Technology and Its Inventions

"By all means, take Steve Humbolt's courses on technology in the science department," so said one of the students, Jerry, who added, "we all love him and his easygoing fascination with new, outside experimental approaches. His class, starting soon, on Technology and Art will be co-taught with Faye Donowitz, of the creative arts department, another popular teacher. They both like to be called by their first names, which helps put everyone at ease."

"I'll enroll right away, thank you," responded Oliver, "as will my companion, Olivia, who is herself a painter."

"Steve is a regular guy, quick to smile and laugh in and outside class, even to be fun and funny."

"What else?"

"Actually, his public persona can be a bit different. Professor or Mr. Humbolt is considered by many outsiders as a bit of a crackpot, coming up with lots of strange bizarre ideas, like transporting or transposing people back and forth through time and space. But he certainly captures our imagination."

"He and Faye sound like a good pair to teach a class like that."

"Yes. So, tell me what you think after the course begins."

"Sure thing."

———————

On the first day of this particular course, the Topping couple went to the front to introduce themselves as auditors to the two teachers and remind Steve about his prior crossing of paths with Oliver years before in California in fleeting exchanges both men by now had almost forgotten (from our preceding two novels). "Some chance encounters in space-time travel?" quipped Steve.

"Possibly so," retorted Olivia, half wondering if this was the start of a new friendship outside class. "Your students quite like your classes."

"Good to hear, thanks." In fact, Oliver remembered from back then how shadowy a figure Steve had seemed but all that was gone by now in the midst of his new-found teaching activities in Boston while each man's continuing interest in new-fangled technologies already augured well.

For her part, Olivia struck up lasting good rapport with fellow art-loving teacher, Faye Donowitz. Exactly what her personal relationship was to Steve Humbolt would remain fairly cloudy. At first, in the class, Faye's artistic input would take a backseat.

———————

"I would like to start," began Steve's initial lengthy lecture, "with a question, hoping for some responses from you all. And the question is: what inventions have fundamentally changed people's lives in the past century or so, which at the time seemed impossible to imagine in importance but eventually became a basic accepted norm of everyday life?"

The class was at first unsure or hesitant to speak up. But with his much older perspective, Oliver started the ball rolling. "Well, in the 19th century came the railroads in England and soon thereafter in America, all as in response to the new age of industrialization and the rise of the factory system and new modes of transportation."

"Good information," prompted the professor, "but what more basic element lay behind all that?"

"The machine itself?" asked the student Jerry.

"Yes, that's right. With new forms of technology came the machine age. Steam engines for locomotives on the railroads for the many thousands of miles of track laid in England and then America in the course of the 19th century. Great British novelists like Charles Dickens and Henry James deplored the social ills and disruptions in everyday life caused by the advent of modern machinery connected with the industrial factory system, despite the great economic advances lauded by so many other writers. This kind of advance in technology and machinery eventually led from the Victorian age to...what else in the early 20th century?"

"Good example would be the airplane, starting with the Wright brothers in the early 1900s and leading roughly only six decades later to landing a man on the moon through rapidly advancing rocketry."

"Good example, Ginger."—another student in the course.

"Thank you, Steve."

"As the machine age advanced (or should we call it the machines' ages because of ever-broadening varieties?), there was an ever increasing dehumanization of everyday life and society into the 20th century. Any further examples?"

"Obviously, the computer age, with the computerization of everyday living and working," prompted student Amanda. "On the other hand, the computer age has brought people together in so many different ways more than ever before through more immediate and instant communication."

From there, the class for that period size of computers in the early 1960s to small hand-held devices a half century later but with more and more people going around inside and outside with their faces glued to their personal phones. A reversion to the earlier machine-era branched out in further directions, with some agreeing that their Emerald College was proof enough of the humanizing effects of modern forms of intercommunication between students and their teachers. Their professor, Steve, took note of the remarkable acceleration of the computer age from the huge room and mentality. From the early steam engines and mechanized society to the modern ages of rocketry and computers.

———

"Now we must briefly introduce," said professor Steve at a subsequent session, "some of the latest forms of 'technology and its inventions', the subject of this course. As we move well into the 21th century, it becomes apparent how much faster the speed of change and advancement is. There seems no limit to how far into the future technological inventions can take us. The changes mankind will take the world in just fifty or one hundred years, let alone in the more distant future become almost impossible to imagine today. But let's look for now at some of the latest inventions impacting everyday life. Who can start us off?"

The students' hands flew up.

"The rapidity of intercommunications is becoming often hard to keep up with," said one student.

"Like what?" asked Steve.

"Like in the digital age," said one student, "there's now the iPhone and iPad moving beyond the Blackberry."

"Also Instagram, Facebook, Twitter, and so forth, with older forms of communication and devices like the fax machine taking a backseat."

"What about the information revolution?" inquired the professor.

Up again flew the hands.

"Especially Google? With it, one can look up almost anything on the World Wide Web."

"Now almost all the world information can be seen in an instant."

"So we see," continued Steve, "how the machine age is still with us, taking us into deeper and deeper depths. The sky seems the limit, no end to the future reality replacing the science fiction of the past, with past, present, and future increasingly intermixed."

"What about space exploration and new forms of technology and inventions?" asked the student already encountered, Jerry.

"Landing a man on Mars in two or three decades will become just as old science as landing a man on the moon, except for the colonies it will generate and continue. What new beyond all that?"

"Now you're asking questions I myself have been asking for some time," said Steve, freely admitting that outsiders have often regarded his ideas as 'crackpot science'.

Jerry immediately spoke up in Steve's defense, "I've already looked into your papers on the 4th and 5th dimensions in which you cite ideas on relativity of time and space in the 4th dimension to show the existence of a 5th dimension in place-time merging past, present, and future."

"Yes, that's it," praised Steve, "but now I'll ask my special colleague, Faye Donowitz, sitting here with me, to explain certain practical applications of this project."

"You all can just call me Faye as well. We're all together in this project. I teach in the art department here at Emerald College, where dreams of the far-out imagination can take off into realms of the real, here and now. For Steve and I are convinced that ways can be found to enable us to transport back or ahead in place and time to meet up with others no longer living or not yet born. I will leave you in suspension on this for now until the next class, in which we'll consider ways we are trying to prove this."

Chapter Three

The Painter's Eye

"What we are seeking," began Faye Donowitz in the next session she and Steve Humbolt taught together on science and art, "is to find an actual mechanism, or medium, for bringing individuals into contact directly with others outside their own immediate outside worlds. The more I look as an art historian at eye contact with the viewers' own eyes, with the artist himself as unseen but real perception and presence, the more I'm convinced here is one way to achieve this goal. Similar ways through art would be to transport one's imagination into other worlds, whether in painting architecture back or ahead into other worlds until the fixation achieves a status of reality beyond what current media are able to achieve. This would go far beyond, say, 'video conferencing' or 'texting' could do.

"Indeed, a new kind of painter's dream machine would have to be invented. Here is where science and art work together in ways that outsiders call 'crackpot science'."

"What the hell are they talking about?" muttered Oliver, half joking to Olivia sitting next to him in the same course as senior auditors.

"Quiet; let's listen and give them a chance. Artists have their fantasies and flights of imagination. Scientists too."

"But—"

"Shush."

"Questions or comments so far?" asked the teacher.

Jerry was quick to respond, as usual. "It sounds to me that you're going in the right direction for today's rapid advancements in technology and its inventions."

"Yes," seconded Amanda, equally talkative. "Think of all the recent inventions like Watson for machinery to develop artificial intelligence, a kind of robot we can interact with even through actual conversation. Watson is real, something science fiction movies could once only speculate about as in the older case of Hal."

Ginger added, "The invention of drones, now ever more widely used in everyday life."

"Anything more about the electronic age," asked Steve.

"Exactly," prompted Faye. "E-commerce, through drone deliveries and mediums like Amazon, is changing or even replacing retail stores and outlets. Someday soon, there will be driverless cars. Even now, airplanes are largely flying automatically by themselves. So the sky seems to be limitless."

"Speaking of that," said Steve, "scientists over at M.I.T. as well as in southern California are already looking ahead to time travel in interstellar space. In other words, concepts and realities of place-time are advancing with space-time. Meaning that we should be able to enter into a new 5th dimension as envisioned in our painter's dream machine."

"It still seems too far-out to me—" But Olivia again motioned Oliver to cease.

More and more in later sessions of the same course, Olivia herself, fellow painter with Claudette Monet and actual mother of Oliver, was speaking up in class about her own viewpoints, which the two professors were eager to hear about.

"A better way to explain this is through thought-time. Eye contact between the painter and the subject being depicted is one very good way to go about doing this, allowing the viewer to step into the scene depicted into the world and communicate directly and personally with the subject being painted. Or in a scene of nature without persons the viewer can walk out into the path leading into the forest beyond.

"Neither I nor Claudette and Claude ever tried to achieve this ultimate effect, but I would like to try or see others now do it. If a kind of device is to be used, it could be a pill or special harmless drug to achieve certain areas of the brain controlling imagination and creative impulses. This could enable the painter's eye to be used in highly sensitive ways to direct human intelligence to enter into new dimensions of place-time along lines we're describing."

By now Oliver was becoming less skeptical, while Olivia was becoming more confident, the class was giving him and her their increasing attention, and both Steve and Faye were nodding their agreement.

The course was really taking off successfully, but was encountering more outside agitation as word of it was filtering out both on and off campus. Steve Humbolt was becoming perceived as evil genius or mad scientist for 'corrupting the youth'. And 'duping the students'. In the meantime, Steve was busy contacting area institutes of technology to see what steps to take in order to conduct experiments designed to show the value and validity of such thinking.

Some encouraging feedback was forthcoming despite ongoing skepticism and negativity in the public press. Oliver Topping himself as former journalist, now retired, was stepping into the fray with a few letters to editors in Boston newspapers, urging development of certain drugs to test the results. Short of finding new specialized drugs, the college administration was urging more immediate experimental tests. Steve and Faye came up with an idea—controversial in part because of the two professors' growing reputations—but nevertheless deemed okay.

Chapter Four

Psychology and Sexuality 101

"The use of drugs to stimulate dreams in the subconscious mind as conveyed in art through requisite procedures is bound to cause some controversy," so said Steve Humbolt in an ensuing session of the same college course he was teaching at Emerald. "This is why I have asked another one of our colleagues who teaches Psychology and Sexuality 101 to make a guest appearance today and explain a few things relating to the subject."

"Good morning, everybody, I'm Tripp Weed, no pun intended even if my friends call me Goodtime Charlie for laughs."

"Oh brother," whispered Olivia to Oliver.

"It's okay," he whispered back.

"Some of you know," Tripp went on, "that the reputed father of modern psychology, Sigmund Freud, wrote *The Interpretation of Dreams*. Can some of you students tell us some of Freud's ideas?"

The hands flew up. Answered some:

"Freud saw dreams as coming from the subconscious mind, what he called the Id, which governs the Ego and even the Superego."

"Aren't dreams a kind of wish fulfillment through which we give free expression to our inner personality seeking some kind of fulfillment?"

"Go on."

"The release of our inner self that often comes out in forms of sexual desire?"

"Freud tended to think our inner personality or Alter ego was able to be controlling as well as controlled by the conscious self through therapy. The question is what kind of therapy."

"Does that mean drugs, and if so, what kind especially by today's standards?" Olivia asked Prof. Weed. "Drug therapy is as old as the hills. Back in the late 1600s in Salem, Mass., it was thought that a 'witch's brew' could help put a 'hex' on people who consumed it. Also, various kinds of marijuana, alias pot or weed, were grown to induce dream-like states of mind for different purposes."

"Around campus here at Emerald," spoke up another student, "most people seem aware of the growing liberality of rules about taking drugs. Lots of hallucinatory effects can follow as with morphine."

Again Prof. Weed, "There are various parts of the brain that respond well to drug-induced dream-like states of mind. Sometimes we have found that experiments with dream therapy of the right kind can cause someone to enter into a place-time fifth dimension comparable to a painter whose imagination is so deeply concentrated on a particular scene as to enable him to be transported or transferred into that medium. But drugs combined with imagination-enhancing locations or settings can be successful in such matters."

Seconded Prof. Humbolt, "We've found in the past that students profit from trips (again no pun intended) to places like Salem, Mass., can be well used to these ends."

"But tell us more about Freud, sexuality, and wish fulfillment," exclaimed a student.

"Well, Freud developed many of his concepts from exchanges with his patients in his Vienna office, particularly women, often Jewish, who happened to have fixations about sex. Dream or wish fulfillment, could seem to suggest, Freud can cause sexual transformation—as in Greek mythology when Hermes and Aphrodite had a son Hermaphrodite whose female lover loved him so much as to cause him to develop both sex organs. Such transformations of people, places, or things can and do occur under right conditions. I leave it to you students and the course head to take further steps and for arranging outside field trips beyond what's available here at Emerald and elsewhere."

"A dream-like state of mind while awake could become a state of reality without being a psychosis might allow the dreamer to enter into that sphere of being so as to enable, for instance, a painter to enter the world or scene he is depicting," according to Prof. Weed, "but we need to conduct further thought experiments into the possibilities of psychological awareness and bodily transformations."

"You mean," asked Olivia, her artist's instinct aroused, "that what is in the beholder's eye can be objectified as well as subjectified? So a man or woman, say, could walk into a real everyday scene and embrace in bodily contact with someone else within the picture or painting? Or in a street scene painted by the Impressionist painter Monet, I, or you could walk in and converse with other strollers?"

"Or even have sex with someone in that other world?" chimed in another classmate.

Now it was Oliver's turn to roll his eyes with skepticism, although willing to hear more.

"That's right," interjected Steve Humbolt. "This is an application of Freud's ideas on dreams as wish fulfillment, in which the subconscious sexuality takes over as conscious reality."

"Is this a drug-induced state of mind?" asked a classmate. "So that fantasy can become reality?"

"Not exactly, but it all depends," responded Tripp Weed.

"What we're getting around to," said Steve Humbolt, "is the need for a short class trip forty minutes away outside Boston to Salem, Mass., and to visit the states of mind there during the famous witch craze of the late 1600s. The college is arranging bus transportation for us to go there during an extended class period, just twenty minutes away."

Chapter Five

Class Trip to Salem

By now, for this popular fall semester course headed by Steve Humbolt, in Salem outside of Boston, it was full-scale Halloween time. Just right for leaps of imagination back into the town's colonial past. Complete with decorations and clothing suggestive of some of the most famous occurrences of the 1690s when witchcraft mania reached its climax in the bizarre trails, holding fascination to the present day.

The trip was well attended by students, visitors, and teachers. After a preliminary tour of the streets, meant to absorb the atmosphere of the place and its historical setting, participants were expected to do their own renderings of Salem scenes and activities to take back to class and explain. After filling in further details.

"The Salem witch trials were the product of dark superstitions about the forces of evil residing in some women and exhibiting bizarre behavior." This was according to Tripp Weed, organizer of the field trip. "Just remember that Freud and others have explored forms of female hysteria and irrational behavior needing treatment or even drugs to control, leaving men sometimes fearful or overwhelmed by these irrational female impulses. Late 19th-century doctors would sometimes attribute sickness to female hysteria, needing rest cure and lots of masturbation. As for witches putting an evil eye on others, even to this day Greeks and many others carry their evil eye objects with them to ward off evil coming from others."

"Tell us more about drugs in old Salem."

"Witches were often thought to grow, consume, and give out all sorts of foods, herbs, and drinks that had effects not unlike marijuana, LSD, or other such mind-altering drugs promoting hallucinations and erratic behavior."

"What happened to those Salem witches?"

"A couple dozen were hung as a result of the trials."

"What about Hawthorne's *Scarlet Letter* about the dark beliefs and behaviors of that period? But Hawthorne's *House of The Seven Gables* was written when he lived in an actual house of that description just down the street where we are standing. It suggests to many observers the very example of a haunted house around this time of year."

"I already feel the presence of supernatural forces around that house," commented Olivia, scrutinizing the house with her discerning artist's eye as the group walked over to the sidewalk in front of the house. Soon others began to notice similar results.

"Curiously enough, we are being trans-morphed into that older thought world. The lunch we ate outside nearby witches museum included some of the very herbs sold there as similar to the very ones potent for mind enhancements for creative imagination, not dangerous or addictive at all."

<hr>

The various student depictions of subjects and scenes from old Salem were soon brought to class for discussion and development. Students found in their own ways that they were able to interact with old Salem as if transported in place and time through some kind of medium they couldn't quite explain.

"Was this related to Freud and other psychologists on the waking dream that takes over from the sleeping dream?"

"Quite possibly," Tripp Weed responded to one such student.

"Or the result of the food or drink we consumed at Salem?"

"Again, quite possibly."

"I still think it was due to concentrated focus of special eye contact that activates the imagination in parts of the brain responsible for creativity and sometimes illusions." So said Steve Humbolt.

"I also agree with Steve's search for some sort of mechanism or medium enabling us to be transported back or ahead in place-time through a new fifth dimension where reality would become more mental and open to infinite universal possibilities." So said Faye Donowitz. "Such a device would hopefully mean we could actually see a person, building, or other subject/ object in the round so we could reach out and actually touch it. The painter's eye could become more powerful than we know."

Once again, Olivia Topping's artistic interests and Oliver Topping's fascination since early youth with experimental technology, as in rocketry, turned them on to all this being said, outweighing some of their skepticism. "Reality can be stranger than fiction," they both agreed.

Their own evocations of old Salem from the class trip there were of much interest. Were their states of mind altered too? Especially like Steve Humbolt's? Were such mental powers and outlooks what had been behind Steve's detractors, not altogether dissimilar to old Salem's residents who feared the forces of evil in the strange unknown?

Chapter Six

Along Commonwealth Avenue

Once back in class from their trip to Salem, teachers and students were fast to reflect on how they felt about being transposed back into that world. Food, drugs, hallucination, waking dream fantasies, and the like were all cited as possible highlights. "But how, to more concretely, to make that inner thought-world an actual present reality?" asked Steve.

"A painter along our Commonwealth Avenue, say, might be able through future technology, be able to transport himself and others, as a physical presence and reality, into that medium. That," according to Faye, "is easy to achieve in would be future technology, even with mechanical devices, relating to a fifth dimension, still to be developed along lines Steve is looking into."

Students readily agreed, as both Oliver and Olivia also assented to, realizing the rapid advancements already being made and their future possibilities not yet imagined. "What the artist's powerful eye can often see enters into another sphere of reality," seconded Olivia.

"Who knows," said Oliver, willing to give all this talk a chance, "maybe even through hand-held devices, much like how early computers were so huge as to fill a large room to the palm-size devices today that store so much more information."

As the class assembled on a plaza of Commonwealth Avenue near the college, intending to cast further light on these forms of reality and unreality in further scenes like those in Salem, a small crowd of local onlookers was gathering to watch and listen, largely out of curiosity about Steve Humbolt's off-campus reputation as a crackpot who was misguiding the impressionable young students. "After all, it had been reported that Humbolt has recently taken students to Salem with talk and practices about witchcraft, hallucinatory drugs, and even entered in."

"He should be reported, along with any other teachers who have taken part in these so-called experiments."

Another on-looker: "Humbolt might even be like a witch himself."

Paying little attention to all these onlooking residents, Steve and the class went on about, this time about Freud and female sexuality as it related to witchcraft and other bizarre forms of sexuality. Once more present, Tripp Weed, whose very name aroused discord among local residents, went on, "Another element behind the Salem phenomenon might be to introduce a form not just of hysteria but of hypnosis, or a trance-like state peculiar to that older place-time period."

"Let's remember, outside here on the darkening fall shadows of Commonwealth Ave., that Freud too had his darkening pervasive nature or subconscious Id. It can prompt bizarre behavior and psychologies. Freud's subjects for his personal patients were typically Jewish women whom he found prone to sexual hang-ups needing therapy, including drugs. They were typically placed on his famed large comfortable well-pillowed couch in his Vienna office conducive for liberating their libido so they could open up for Freud to analyze. A kind of hypnotism could be generated, even though many might disagree but helping to account for the Salem craziness of the past—and present. But let's get on with our mini walking tour here on historic Commonwealth Ave."

The crowd of on-looking locals was growing, minded to report all this to the authorities.

"What do you see now in line with our experiences in old Salem?"

"I see shadows falling all around us here," exclaimed one student.

Another: "I see moving old Victorian brownstones almost haunting me, row after row, stoop after stoop, block after block all along outside here in mesmeric motions."

Another: "I feel I can walk all around these streets darkened by dusk and shadows, and actually interact in the round, not just on a flat painting surface, with people once living here many years ago in the Victorian Age when things were so different from now."

"Good to hear all of you students and others going along with this. We would like you to capture these scenes and images in your follow-up drawings or paintings," encouraged Faye Donowitz.

By now, the gathering locals were muttering among themselves about Steve Humbolt and the other teachers for corrupting the youth and encouraging psychotic behavior through illicit means.

"He should be reported."

"Or locked up?"

"Throw away the key."

On-campus reactions were muted, whether in the student newspaper or the administrations responses. At most there was regarded by detractors as a harmless crackpot. Nevertheless, was Steve onto something that could well develop into something significant with application to a place-time fifth dimension not as yet noticed or accepted by the wider scientific community? Or just reducing to a crackpot professor's right to freedom of speech?

Chapter Seven

Double Dealings

But wait!

It turned out that Steve Humbolt had a checkered past that was catching up to him, after many years of eluding identification and prosecution. He had once been tied to several crimes in California including theft, drug trafficking, and murder. Despite his potentially important work on place-time applications in a fifth dimension, he had a psychological problem. He had a kind of double personality that he himself accepted as evidence of a Freudian split personality, in which his dominant ego had another alter ego sometimes able to override it and take control temporarily, with negative results. Perhaps this was one reason behind his fascination with the old Salem witch trials.

For many Salem residents back then, the witches (with their prolonged convoluted spells) had both rational peaceful traits of personality as well as tendencies regarded as evil and dangerous, haunted by demons needing to be cast out even by public execution to ward off evil spirits further infecting the community at large that in cases where ordinary exorcism had proved unsuccessful.

Steve sometimes justified this contorted double contorted personality to himself by looking to other such forces represented in literature and music. The doppelganger or double-goer in German literature was an example. Phantom doubles sometimes makes appearances in Dickens' novels. Brainology would have other viewpoints.

Even though Steve accepted his own double personality as a fixed fact, he believed it could not only be manageable through therapy, but also, in the infinite possibilities of future advanced technology, be used to enable face-time with space-time between painted people and their outside observers. Hence, his quest took on another more personal imperative.

———————

"Oliver, I'm beginning to remember how you and I crossed paths briefly with Steve Humbolt when you came to California years ago to see me and Claudette there. I knew I'd seen him somewhere before."

"I don't recall, Olivia."

"Sure you do. You even interviewed him for one of your news articles as correspondent covering that infamous murder case near Hollywood."

"You mean, the Mansoni murder of two famous female actresses?"

"Yes."

"How so?"

"Steve had been implicated in the get-away car."

"Oh yes. That was long before I retired as a reporter."

"He looked much different back then, with long hippie hair and wrinkled clothes. His case was dropped later but there were lingering suspicions. He maintained his innocence but seemed slightly delusional. He had interesting stories to tell about his life in hippie communes that Mansoni was also a big part of. He seemed to be on some kind of hallucinatory drug or food. A little spaced out but hard to tell exactly what was going on with Steve."

"Another even briefer contact as well, not on that case?"

"Yes."

"Do you think he has remembered us in our audit of his Emerald class?"

"Maybe, but hard to tell." Oliver shrugged. "But he's made comments in class about the Boston strangler case, saying he has 'had experience with such delusional deranged killers before', while adding that such types must be guarded against and not listened to no matter how rational they come across."

"Steve has also said he once talked to the police handling that Boston case. I guess he's not worried about the college administration here connecting these two cases, considering his reputation as a far-out professor."

"I guess not."

"I hope if he ever develops an interactive painter's dream machine that the viewer of a particular painting will not find figures leaping out at him."

"Yes," laughed Oliver.

Dealing with Steve's double persona was becoming more difficult, harmless though it seemed to his admiring students if they noticed its signs at all, until his public perception was catching up with his campus popularity and causing the administration to step in with whatever remedy they could muster. Then the problem escalated as he began speaking out in class about it, riling up the students on his behalf. His student Jerry was especially vocal in Steve's defense. But who was this standout Jerry anyway?

"I'm related to Steve Humbolt and know him to be a worthy sane person. All this gossip about him being a demented schizophrenic with harmful split personality is just that, gossip, nothing more. Some outsiders are just jealous about his popularity and significant ideas and quest for practical applications. In this age of infinite possibilities for the future, the sky is limitless."

"How are you related to him?"

"There is still some uncertainty, but we are still trying to learn if he is my biological father from California and if Faye here is my biological mother."

Now things were really heating up. And with that bit of revelation, Oliver and Olivia perked up, considering their own backgrounds.

"Perhaps Steve's painter's dream machine will help find answers," sympathized fellow student Amanda.

Likewise too supportive was Ginger, who naively remarked, "Don't worry, Steve, those murder mysteries some people are whispering about you are all crazy talk."

"Yeah," agreed other classmates. And there such talk ended for now at vacation time.

Part Two

Proving the Machine

Chapter Eight

Vacation Assignment

With the long intersession vacation now approaching, Steve Humbolt and Faye Donowitz began preparing their students in Boston's Emerald College course to do a special project report testing the validity of a painter's dream machine with direct intercommunication between painter and his subject through direct eye contact.

"We want you," said Steve, "to go to an accessible area museum, using the chemical compounds and special glasses provided for you, which should be returned along with your specified final report."

"We are also giving you all," added Faye, "a special note in case you need it for identification purposes; again, if you need one in the course of your investigations. You can contact either one of us if you need to."

Off soon went Oliver and Olivia to visit friends in New York City. For him, it was a return to old familiar haunts. For her, this was a relative new experience, but with strange portents of oddities about to occur that never were, while seeming reminiscent of other times and places.

From his earlier years in New York City, Oliver had befriended and kept in touch with some staff members of the Metropolitan Museum of Art, where he himself had once worked part-time as a nighttime security guard to earn extra money. There, his imagination had often gone rampant with visions of long-departed people and scenes portrayed by the wide assortment of painters. Of particular fascination now were the 19th-century galleries, featuring paintings by artists like Monet, Renoir, Seurat, Pissarro, and other notables centering around Monet and the Impressionists and their kind. Walking the corridors, once again alone at night, through special access, the viewer was filled with strange encounters.

Suddenly, the darkened interior spaces of the galleries lit up brightly, revealing two couples, as if in Édouard Manet's Impressionist-era *Luncheon On The Grass* (see Google image). Two well-attired men and one naked woman sit or recline on the grass alongside a public park path, having munch, while a background woman bends over washing herself. The naked woman looks at you, the viewer, approaching the group.

Manet's painting was acquiring a new dimension. "What's your problem?" queries the naked woman. "Haven't you ever seen a nude woman before?"

"Well, actually, not like this."

"How so?"

"It's just so stark and public of a contrast. If we ever tried to do this in Boston where I'm from. Or especially Iowa where I grew up, I'd be put in jail."

"That sounds like Salem witch trial country."

"Precisely."

"What are you doing here in liberal-minded France if you're going to be so prudish in your American ways?"

"It's the same kind of illicit prostitution ring open to public acceptance and involvement?"

By now, viewer and participant are already becoming confused over who, what, and where all this is taking place.

"What's your problem?" inquired the nude lady sitting on the grass in the public park with the other figures. In so doing, she stood up and walked over to the viewer(s) in the foreground just outside the picture frame. "Go away and leave us alone," she added.

A small crowd soon gathered around the group. The park's police arrived, seeing nothing unusual or objectionable. The group soon dispersed and disappeared. After the American interlopers from Boston gave their ID and contact information to the authorities, in fact they were the ones disturbing the peace and not those on the grass who by now had all taken their clothes off in support of Manet's naked woman and her public rights to be so.

"What is going on?" complained an official back at Boston's Emerald College. Local opinion inside and outside the college there was agitated as more and more incidents like the above were being transmitted to the interested parties via all sorts of futuristic technologies increasingly available, accompanied by growing complaints against the evils of such devices. Another round of Old Salem-like witch trials seemed ever more possible. Suspicions were growing.

"To make matters worse," voiced the local gossip-mill about Emerald, "Steve Humbolt and crew were now in supposed communication with the mother of the two young children in another painting by Renoir showing the children both wearing long dresses sitting next to their mother on couch, with intimations of the boy's transgenderism, something abhorrent to Old Salem-like mentalities, but acceptable to later progressive social thinking."

"The ever expansive evils inherent in modernistic technologies and their social consequences are becoming unbearable," declared an old diehard conservative around about Emerald College, "not to mention the self-proclaimed ability to communicate with persons in a painting through newfangled electronic devices."

"But," voiced another oldster, "surely someday, eventually, all things are possible."

Chapter Nine

Night Watch

"**A** trance-like inducement of alternative reality is now taking over, making it difficult to tell clearly who is speaking what to whom. Is this a multi-layered dialogue or a perplexing monologue? The stage of dreaming is indeterminate. But wait. For a painter to communicate with the subject being portrayed is said to require a special kind of dream machine best operating at night when mystery combines with imagination and infinite possibilities."

"Mystique, mistiness, and mystery help draw the viewer into the world of the figures or scenes being depicted by the painter. Impressionism and Neoimpressionism in Monet, Manet, Renoir, and Seurat provide examples."

"Direct eye contact between painter and subject painted can be found in earlier works by David, Ingres, Vermeer, Rembrandt, and others. But the dynamic results for present depictions of the painter's dream machine are best vividly evident through Impressionism."

"For us painters of Impressionist styles, it was the retreat out-of-doors, from indoor studios into the world of nature that is most compelling. But a natural world made up of often misty fragmented impressions as if in a dream, where reality itself can seem as much fantasy as the real thing, almost other worldly. Our Monet is emblematic. His faces look at us through the day mists of nighttime.

"Your new hand-held mechanical devices here in the museum enable you to highlight paintings all over the world as never before. And to enter into our world of long ago, to intercommunicate with us no matter how surreal. Monet's objects in nature have a roundness that draws one out into the world beyond.

"In different fashion, the tubular figures of Seurat's Neoimpressionism his phantom figures, with their misty silhouettes as in Seurat's *La Grande Jatte* have a compelling mystery all their own, out of doors yet in a night vision. Here shadows have a luminosity of their own, with which to guide one in between the worlds on display." (See Google image.)

"Through hypnotic self-propulsion brought about best at night while alone, the viewer should become able, with proper mechanisms and chemicals, to move into or with the painter's depictions of movements. Come join us as we move into and along with the shadowy fleeting impressions of dancers in Degas renderings beckoning us to enter in.

Why should not Degas' dancers move in and out between their world and ours, given the proper conditions of advanced electronic technology and chemical compounds? The same should apply to our ability to move further along the path in Edouard Manet's *Luncheon on the Grass* (see Google image), the nude woman looks back at us with expectant eyes as we advance further toward her into her space."

"Does all this mean that spirits or corporeality's of people long ago deceased can somehow be brought back to life, whether from a painting, statue, religious creed, or whatever? Why not? Such occurrences have long ago been claimed by some. What about the ancient Egyptians? Let us walk further around these nighttime galleries and reflect on the wider time travels they could inspire for us. Who or what calls out to us from tombs, statuary, inscriptions, decorations, mummies, sarcophagi, etc.? And what about the pyramid with a lit-up eyeball top at the apex on the U.S. dollar bill, a commanding energy to guide us in the dark? Is it not an ultimate living presence of the ancient all-seeing Egyptian eye at the shining pyramidal apex in a US dollar bill that suggests an ultimate energy for a new order across the ages?"

Chapter Ten

Gothic Ghosts

Classic poetic lines by T.S. Eliot are again apropos. "Let us go then, you and I when the evening is spread out before the sky, like a patient etherized upon a table."

Is the night watch experienced by solitary strollers through the museum in search of a proven dream machine an etherized alternative reality involving their conscious and unconscious minds interfuse to form new intercommunication between the living and those deceased?

Or is a gothic ghost also appearing? A spirit and form of persons from times past coming back to haunt those still present? And especially in eerie places and settings? Evocations of dark late Victorian, and even earlier Romantic, auras can erupt? As in Gothic horrors by Henry James?

"So let us go then, you and I, from museum to old haunts long since gone by, to see what now will strike the eyes. Would it be, as for Ezra Pound's poetry, that the crowds' facts would become dark apparitions? Up by Columbia, across 121 St., next to Teacher's College and Union Theological Seminary, the eyes from decades past still stare out with Victorian Gothic intensity. But ghosts often vanish when stared back at. Observing the scene intently with the painter's eye can bring new views more agreeable."

"Old long-forgotten street scenes further along upper Broadway come back from etherized memory to haunt with supernatural visions. Do we dare to enter into an old apartment dwelling now vacant with unlocked door for real estate brokers to show prospective tenants? Us ghostly apparitions are once again peering at you with hypnotic stares through moving subway escalator windows into your Harlem windows."

"Look now at the whispering ethereal, transforming, eye staring at us from atop the great pyramidal apex, all lit up to shine forth its hypnotic spell."

"You will look for me, and you will find us, when you search for us in all the old familiar places where you once lived and thrived here in New York. Our ghosts can still be summoned forth in response to paintings of communicated as if in dreams of Claudette Monet or Oliver."

Our painter's eye calls forth a compelling vision to enter into the scene of the supernatural. Paintings by Olivia Topping, as painter herself, would be a natural medium to turn these past images into communicable realities.

Chapter Eleven

Corrupting the Youth

"These kinds of unusual and uncertain futuristic happenings by our students during their vacation assignments are no hoax or joke." So reported Steve Humbolt along with Faye Donowitz to the upset Emerald College president, the usually ultra-liberal Snead Zwerling.

"Maybe so," said Snead, "but I have been getting a number of bad feedback from sources here in Boston and elsewhere including New York."

"Like what?"

"Like two of your student adult auditors who, with others, claim powers to bring back the dead in picture galleries and on the street."

"That's a wild exaggeration of what they are doing. A mischaracterization."

"Maybe so, but it's causing bad publicity for the college and my administration, perhaps including admissions and student enrollment."

"The ultra-conservative area residents are taking up the issue," added one of Snead's assistants, "more than is warranted. They sound off like old Salemites, ranting as if chanting against our so-called crackpot professors."

"Very anti-futuristic technology," said another administrator at the meeting.

"Freedom of speech is one thing," said the president, "but some crazy witchcraft types are compelling us to Socrates. 'Corrupting the youth' with his far-out ideas."

Steve and Faye held their peace for the time being.

Boston at the time was full of conflicting forces of good and evil. Snead Zwerling seemed the perfect embodiment of this combination. "I'm a lover of Boston's old historic traditions," he told his friends, "but I need to escape from their constrictions and to seek radical new directions. I despise racism and anti-Semitism; but I feel it's wrong to deny Boston's rich historical heritage of Anglo-Saxon Waspy Puritanism," as Snead elaborated.

Among the often criticisms of Emerald College voiced by nearby residents was that it was "liberally too prone to crazy ideas", as one longtime elderly neighbor complained, "too disruptive of normal conservative values."

Part, no doubt, of this local criticism was anti-Semitism toward college staff and implicit bias against perceived 'corruption of the youth', by such popular professors as Steve Humbolt, as pointed out by one of his colleagues.

"Some of the ultra-conservative local residents around Emerald," reported a Boston newspaper, "feel so threatened by a student body radicalized by their liberal teachers and staff that they're ready to take action. Old Salemite and

Puritan traditions are again coming together into conflict with newer ultra-liberalism."

Emerald's Snead Zwerling warned his staff and faculty to "be on the lookout for signs of Boston mob interference in these matters. The Boston mafia is in our midst living and hanging out in conservative old enclaves like this."

"How so?" asked the director for community affairs, Donna Brazil.

Answered Snead Zwerling, "The Boston Irish mob keeps a lower profile than the New York mob. New York mob is more aligned with the Italian Catholic church and more liberal doing so-called public good works there but with publicity on its criminal hits and hangouts. The Boston Irish mob is still tied to old Salemite conservative areas like ours in Boston and vicinity.

"So, they sometimes are called upon to do the dirty work in neighborhood disputes of more personal conflicts. Puritan era witch trials and hangings still excite their imagination. Our college could become an easy target. To be seen as guarding against corruption of the youth could be perceived as a good-faith public work in their mind."

Chapter Twelve

Evils of Automation

Further dark forces of stormy conflict were gathering around and near Emerald College along Boston's Commonwealth Ave. For Oliver and Olivia Topping, now in their second semester as senior auditors, even the surrounding architecture of the old dark late-Victorian revival styles and brownstone facades were acquiring new hauntings of their own.

"It seems like our past lives are coming back to haunt us in some bizarre mixture, as if in some witch's brew intensified by our surroundings."

"I know what you mean, Oliver," said Olivia.

"But we've come such a long way together, haven't we?"

"What does it all mean?"

"I wish our old inner selves could still be helped along by our dear Claudette Monet."

"At some point, we should travel to Paris to look for those old paintings she once did, to see if any of them include self-portraits we could activate for direct contact with her, like we've already tried to do electronically with other subjects."

"I feel we came close to that in New York haunts at night, with Claudette's apparition close by."

"Someday!"

"But right now, so many evils seem to be taking over."

"The evils of today, in the midst of ultra-conservative neo-Salemites and neo-Puritans still haunted by inner demons, are not so different from those in the past."

"How so?"

"We've already seen how advances in technology have brought many criticisms. Back in the 19th century, it was the ills of the machine age and industrialization that bothered writers like Dickens and Henry James. Not long after you and I were born around 1940, came huge advances in technology. Now the advancements in computers and electronics have gone so far as to make the old guard people still with us to feel threatened and reactionary. What we are witnessing."

"Right now, as we speak," cautioned Snead Zwerling at a faculty meeting about the growing incitements of conflict, "there is the real danger of riots and violence.

"This sounds like the English Luddites of the 19th century who felt so threatened by the advent of the age of industry, the machine, and steam power, that they went around breaking apart and destroying factory machinery. Railroads were another evil target for them."

To the reborn Salemite mind at that point, evils of all sorts lurked in dark corners everywhere, like witches of old. Amid the old Victorian brownstone walkup buildings along with, modernism and progressivism, something sinister seemed on the verge of happening. Dark clouds around Commonwealth Ave. and Emerald College were threatening new horrors, new destructions.

One afternoon, an alert went out to beware the alien drone creatures hovering about in the skies around that area. Automated drones, dark and forbidding, were hovering overhead, some bumping into the taller buildings while others were landing on the ground. Some people were picking up the newfangled electronic phones and talking to people on these electronic hand-held devices. Still others were picking up packages mailed to them. Soon iPhones and Instagram were everywhere, bringing automations of unusual kinds. People were soon communicating with each other, using these contraptions while looking down at the ground like strange animals and not looking up or even with each other, including standing in public in dark corners and alleyways. The electronic age and computerized humanity were bringing threats to old ways.

At the forefront of the ensuing conflicts between old customs and new innovations were colleges like at Emerald in the Boston area, heavily aligned with new technology institutes, now doing battle with enemies of "progress." The Luddites of old were again trying to break up the new machinery they so detested and feared. The Salemites living in the midst of the wider Emerald community were breaking into buildings and destroying property. They were enlisting the help of the Boston mafia, who once again had their own source of drugs to keep the action flowing with dark images of forbidden forms and figures.

63

Chapter Thirteen

Psychic Eye Powers

"Another big driving force for these neo-Salemites in their hatred of modernism is the element of all things supernatural."

"How so?" Olivia responded to Oliver. "I would think the supernatural could help rather than hurt them."

"The modern computer, which has spanned the information age, has also brought us all ahead to the promise of artificial intelligence."

"And…"

"And that could help give us greater psychic powers as we look ahead to the future as well as the past."

"And that could give more promise for some than the machine held out for others in the 19th century such as Salemites and Luddites."

"Okay," agreed Olivia. "Even so, the proximity of Emerald and other Boston area colleges to high tech technology companies and all their futuristic products makes Salemites of today feel threatened in their conservative ways."

"If we look far ahead," mused Oliver, "we can imagine new technologies enabling mankind to have settlements on

Mars and even to travel outside our solar system. The ability to do all this would bring with it psychic powers to communicate with space aliens and intelligent beings in other dimensions in the universe."

"So the idea of communicating with figures present in a painting through special wiring and special chemical, is not as implausible as many might think."

"Dream parapsychology would also be by then sufficiently advanced to enable this."

"Precisely."

<hr>

Meantime, the Topping twosome, still undefined in their newer relationship since earlier times, continued on with their explorations into psychic phenomena even while the conflicting forces of good and evil were embroiling Boston.

In their continuing search for the real visage and embodiment of their deceased Claudette Monet, using their newly developed futuristic media, the pair went even deeper into Impressionist painting of the later 19th century. Salemite community and Emerald's seething cauldron were receding? Talking as they walked through the available collections:

"I remember Claudette telling me, in those California years I spent as a painter with her, about the great Claude Monet. After whom she was named."

Oliver noted, "How Claude Monet's brush strokes gave fleeting impressions rather than solid outlines, unlike previous paintings. His landscape scenes gave fresh outdoor looks into misty mysterious sketchy worlds, drawing the viewer deeper beyond his present world. Through his misty scenes Monet's people often look through the viewer's eyes, both sides looking deep into the other, transfixed."

"As a neo (or post) Impressionist painter," added Olivia, "George Seurat went further into the mysterious movements of his subject's psychic almost trance-like state of being. His *Circus Sideshow* and *La Grande Jatte* (see Google image) take us into another world of existence haunted by the alternate universe and dimension. They frequent feature tubular automated robotic figures. His thousands of dots, different from Monet's brush strokes give deeper mistiness to penetrate."

By now, who was speaking what to whom and with what effect? The misty narcotic smells of Seurat's gas lighting in *Circus Sideshow* blend with Eliot's patient etherized upon a table in his *Prufrock* to envelop Eliot's women walking to and fro in a museum at night in that poetry, also blending with Monet's misty impressions more generally, all communicating back and forth with us. And linking viewer and subject depicted.

Chapter Fourteen

The Ghost of Claudette Monet

Soon began returning, first in and around Boston. Those already aware of her looks from pictures associated with her celebrated case knew full well what to be on the lookout for because of what this meant.

Calling for school to be in lockdown, Snead Zwerling and other Emerald officials cautioned everyone there to report any such sightings.

"By now, a painter much like Claudette, I'm able (Olivia) to do paintings of Claudette that conjure forth the exact image of Claudette, with whom we need to communicate, while ingesting the same chemical compounds we (Oliver and I) did on our New York trip." So wrote Olivia to her two Emerald professors Steve Humbolt and Faye Donowitz, who had taught her class so well in the technical and artistic methods needed.

"So far, our painter's dream machine is off to a good start," said Faye.

"The day will come in the distant future that communications with extraterrestrial beings will bring us into all kinds of new dimensions," declared Steve.

At this point, a horde of agitated Salemite Luddites were breaking into the Emerald rooms where such conversations were occurring—smashing things up as they rampaged.

"I don't condone any of this bad activity," exclaimed Claudette's increasingly visible apparition as she moved around. "This is not the serene peaceful world I have inhabited as Claude Monet's namesake."

"Emerging from the paintings into the 4th and 5th dimensions, Claudette was starting to perplex and scare those who had lately brought her back into new life.

"She's like the genie who could not be put back into the bottle after being created from it," one observer commented.

"Or have the Salemite-Luddites been right all along," spoke another, "by warning against the evils of automated creatures coming to modern life in the forms of robots, e-books, drones, driverless cars, and with much worse to come not yet invented?"

"Is this woman coming to us as a monster out of a dark forbidden background?"

"What next? The ominous mafia to spreading evil further around?"

Indeed, the French mafia was becoming the secret source for the undisclosed chemical compound used to help the painter's dream machine to bring people to life as in Steve's and Faye's experiments. This meant a French connection had to be explored in depth. It also meant exploring Claudette's French background to understand her own natural artistic abilities in this content, along with those of her close younger follower, Olivia Topping.

When the ghost of Claudette Monet now appeared or reappeared in France, she was again met with great public consideration. The forces of evil met together as one in the French, Boston, and New York mafias in search of the new drugs for the dream machine to help others experience similar results.

"I'm coming to you all here at water's edge on the beach painted by my grandmaster Claude himself," said Claudette.

"Threaten to shoot her if Claudette won't tell us how to get the drugs and construct the machine," said one mobster.

"No go," said another, "she's a ghost and will just vanish before we can get the secret out of her."

By now, the ghost of Claudette Monet was more decisive. "If you want to find the main source of supply for the chemical compound in the dream machine, you'll have to go to Claude Monet's Giverny gardens in Normandy and speak to both of us there as we appear to you through our faces through animated brush stroke impressions filling the large painting set up for you there."

Another kind of Normandy invasion then soon appeared. "I see hordes of mafia invaders descending upon Monet's Giverny gardens, expecting to find the chemical compounds growing naturally for the dream machine," so spoke another ghost from out of the new dimensions.

Then appeared out of the Impressionistic haze another kind of robotic creature. "The stiff stick figures are coming out of Seurat's paintings to invade us en masse," according to yet another ghostly voice. "The figures in Seurat's *Circus*

Sideshow and *La Grande Jatte* (see Google image) are overwhelming us with their scary robotic figures coming out to haunt us, all like invading armies marching toward us."

How would all this end, or wouldn't it? Once the genie has been released from the bottle, can it be put back?

Chapter Fifteen

Voices from Beyond in Streams of Consciousness

"**O**ur beginnings and endings flow together into one stream and many streams."

"How true, Oliver," said Olivia. "But who are we, separate or together?"

"The same question goes for our dear Claudette Monet."

"I know."

"And for Steve Humbolt and Faye Donowitz in relation to their student Jerry."

"True."

"The same might also be said of our reputed parents, Henry and Alice Topping."

"True again."

"Where is all this leading?"

"Or Steve Humbolt and the killer Mansoni?"

"How does all this fit into ideas of split personalities and double persona?"

"That psychologist Dr. Huckabe was a believer in Monet's drug therapy through his home garden products in France. The chemical compounds allowing us to meet up and talk with persons portrayed in paintings, including those by himself. All real or just imagined?"

"I wonder where all that leaves Salemite Luddites antagonists?"

"Psychic paranormal phenomena do occur. Dr. Huckabe accepted Harvard's William James, who argued for validities of ghosts coming back in the present world to unnerve us."

"When we see the ghost of Claudette Monet, are we also able to see the ghost of her namesake, Claude Monet? Why not? After all, Claude is calling beyond the grave for us to come visit."

"Tell us more about your relationships with Faye and Steve in the past, prior to having them as our class teachers at Emerald," asked Ginger innocently but also naively. "How could you say in front of our class that they might be your parents?"

"It shouldn't surprise you, Ginger, that many of us here have had lots of free love and free sex in our lives now and in the past," explained Jerry. "Many of us aren't always sure who are parents and grandparents are."

"Wow," replied Ginger.

"A pretty girl like you has not had sex before now?"

"Well, no, at least not all the way with intercourse."
"Maybe you need to find the right guy to be your first guy…"

"Maybe so…"

"What about the two of us…?"

"Let's try using Steve's chemical compound for stimulating otherworldly visions," asked Ginger, now excited.

They gave each other the chemicals to consume, giving them unusual feelings of intense perception.

"Let's try it front, back, oral, anal, every which way."

"Yes," agreed Ginger.

Resulting commotions were coming to the attention of not only their teachers, Steve and Faye, but also the surrounding neighborhoods as well as wider school population.

Criticisms and repercussions were flying all around. Investigations of Steve and Faye were mounting. College President Snead Zwerling found that using the 'painter's eye' method himself, he could discern Jerry's true origins as child of both Steve and Faye, both now coming to light out of a deep dark background.

"It turns out," reported Zwerling, "that users of the same painter's eye as the Topping pair here have learned Jerry's identity as the child of Steve and Faye resulted from one of their past sexual contacts with each other."

Then Oliver and Olivia Topping did more of their own investigations into their own past and identity.

"It never had been clear whose child Oliver Topping truly was," said another voice. "But now, using our painter's eye and improved dream machine, we're convinced that neither Henry nor Alice were ever our birth parents to begin with back in Iowa." So said Oliver, with Olivia's agreement, speaking with Dr. Huckabe still in Iowa as an elderly psychologist with whom they had worked.

As we know from the previous second novel in this trilogy, Claudette Monet was the true birth mother of one Topping 'twin' while a non-related other 'twin' was the true birth father. Sexual encounters were at the crux in each case, leaving aside Henry and Alice Topping; such that the originally supposed 'twins' were not related by blood at all.

"So where does all this leave us now?" asked Oliver and Olivia to each other.

"After all these years together, shouldn't we finally be married?"

"Agreed. We should have a small ceremony here at Emerald."

"Too bad we never had children of our own. Or have we?"

"A student like Amanda here would have been a wonderful daughter. Let's use our painter's dream machine with painter's eye to communicate with dear Claudette Monet to find our best solutions. Who knows if we already have such a person in, say, Amanda?"

"The possibilities for artificial intelligence in the ever expanding computer machines seem endless, limitless, even as infinite as the universe itself."

"Yes, the voices able to talk, communicate, and interact with each other are already being explored at places like M.I.T. no longer mere ghost-like but on new verges of reality."

———————

As we remember from the first novel in this trilogy, the background and life of Claudette Monet went back a long often mysterious way, leaving some topics not fully resolved. For instance, in the previous second novel, who was the illegitimate father in New Jersey of Henry Topping's cousin's teenage daughter who gave birth to a son who was switched at the last minute at birth and given as a newborn to Henry and Alice in Iowa to help create the Topping 'twin' story and make up for their former lost still-born Topping twin from long before? Newer 'intelligence' helped resolve this.

And what more about Claudette Monet's American father from Pennsylvania who died early in his life (first novel) never really identified? Or the pseudonym Claudette Monet given to her by her mother back in France to give her the notoriety of the famous unrelated painter Claude? In the end, elaborate entangled mysteries must sometimes leave matters partly unresolved. The free imagination still carries forth beyond what dared not to be entered into. Would advanced artificial intelligence come someday at a steep price and with heavy disruptions?

Part Three

Painterly Dreams in a Novelesque Phantasmagoria

We now turn, in different ways, to a novel-like story within our wider novel (a shorter novella within a longer novel) in ways not usually encountered. The preceding accounts of Old Salem ghosts and phantasmagorias can here be brought to life through pictorial fantasies in Gothic architecture and other mediums.

Through artificial intelligence, we have just seen some of the endless possibilities of physic phenomena. Here, then, are some further constructions. A disjunctive style helps convey the tenor and mental state of the protagonist.

I

The lone majestic flow of the River Rhone has for many centuries been a source of wonderment and legend for the German imagination transfixed by its myriad special geographic features embedded in the German psyche.

On its flow northward, eventually out into the sea, the River Rhone receives in turn smaller tributaries following in and down with it, such as at Cologne (in the French or Koeln as in the German), depending on which nation was controlling.

The overall effect is one of dynamic energy but also one of serene contemplation, or of something soon to happen.

For those sightseeing in this area, one of the prime attractions has long been the Cologne Cathedral. It's a massive soaring stone structure and presents itself at a foreboding, some might say sinister, remainder of Gothic horror stories associated with the phantasmagoria horror ghost stories of older times, going back in particular to Germany in the 18th century. This phantom-like eerie spirit has in more recent ages been by the destruction caused by the bombing of World War 2. But the particular enormity of the German Gothic designs of Cologne Cathedral, once the biggest, tallest building in Europe, has forever contrasted with the refined graceful French Gothic designs of Chartres and Notre Dame in France, protecting a much different non-threat.

Where the Cologne Cathedral stands on the eastern side of the Rhine is roughly less problematic in German history than is on the other side, which came to be called the Rhineland westward toward France. The Rhineland became a kind of demilitarized zone in the aftermath of World War I. But in the 1930's, Hitler invaded and took back the Rhineland, a major step into a French invasion and point of no return toward much broader take overs. With terrible outcomes for all Europe, including for the Cologne Cathedral and environs.

As the story unfolds from a regular sightseeing trip into a different kind of fantasy with a ghost-like presence, too easily achieved through special effects of lighting.

The young man, Dietrick Knoblock, arrived by train alone at night in Cologne, his first time there near where he was born. Dark lonely shadows hung around city lightning with dim sparse, somehow a reminder of past war time conditions of foreboding.

The Cathedral's dominating structure right in with its Gothic solemnity, was punctuated by small disks of surrounding house lights. Still hung heavy with the very air still hung with the suspiciousness left over from the war and its long aftermath. The partly deserted night-time streets gave shadowy accents to the still bombed out portions of the stark structure of the German feature of the Gothic Cathedral; its top-heavy facade and body haunching over the scene like some giant Sphinx.

II

As was his habit, sightseeing through Germany, Dietrick usually found youth hostels and similar places to spend the adventurous spirit and meeting with the locals. But on this night, his train having been late on arrival, this dark setting found him out of sorts on where to stay. So, he did the next best thing under the conditions and found his way to the local police station to inquire on what to do as a total stranger. To his surprise and relief, he found the officials there to be helpful and engaging, not quite like the Gothic horror tale he had been expecting; even if with a touch of German formality.

"Hi, officer, I'm Dietrick Knoblock. My train is arriving late and I have nowhere to stay tonight. Could you please tell me where I could find a place to stay to spend the night?"

"Unfortunately," replied the officer, "all is locked up or closed at this hour."

"Should I go back and sleep in the station?"

"That is forbidden due to tight security."

"No public space to stretch out on?"

"That is correct. Forbidden."

"What to do? How about here?"

"What? Well, I could put you in a jail cell to keep you off the streets… Okay. I will lock you in for the night. I will give you some food and drink I keep here for strangers."

"Thank you, officer."

"My name is Wilhelm Franck, chief officer at this station."

"Thanks again, Wilhelm."

"Who are you, anyway, so I know? Are you German?"

"My ancestry is very German on both my father's and mother's sides. But I have never been to Germany before this summer trip."

"So, you're an American with a solid German first and last name.

"Let me tell you something. Be very careful about saying you're American in the condition Germany is in today. Your name is a good thing. But remember that many Germans still dislike America because of America's defeat of Germany so soon after World War II. Occasional acts of anti-American violence still do occur. So, this means watching out for your safety too."

"How do people of Cologne feel today about the heavy American bombing of the Cathedral?"

"Lots here see their beautiful Cathedral as a hateful desperation, always center stage before them daily. So be careful and watch out."

The next day, Dietrick soon met up with some other sightseers from other countries who all spoke enough German and English to get by okay. Through them, he learned of the rectory lodging available at the Cathedral as a new temporary facility to help defray costs of reconstructing the bombed-out edifice. The rector in charge spoke with the group, welcoming them with a little accounting of Cathedral history, now with a curious twist.

"Your name, Dietrick Knoblock, reminds me of a Cologne hero in the War who was killed by the Nazi soldiers during the Allied bombing of Cologne and it's Cathedral where we now standing."

"I'm not aware of any such connection. Must be a different Dietrick Knoblock."

"When the Allies were bombing us here, many once pro-Hitler people began to see that Hitler was bringing us into ruin by pursuing a wider war and persecuting the Jews, and many were turning against Hitler."

"Yes, said one of the other sightseers, some heroic Germans actually tried to save a crucial bridge near here across the Rhine so Allied troops could cross and go on to Berlin to defeat Hitler and the War."

"And," said the church rector, "Dietrick Knoblock, who at first had been pro-Hitler, led the Germans trying to save the bridge for the Allies, was eventually killed by the Nazis for his key role in all of this."

"What before then?"

"He had a son, likewise named Dietrick Knoblock."

A search of the Cathedral and city records indicated that a son (or grandson, the records were partly unclear and damaged) had been taken after the War, to America but without any further clarification except that he was taken in (or adopted?). The records may be altered to show up as a pro-Nazi past but again, that is ambiguous. Further, lost in the haze of very early childhood consciousness were details of our Dietrick Knoblock for the first time confronted by a complex family's secret past.

Would he ever get to the real bottom of it all?

85

III

"Meanwhile," cautioned the rector, "it is getting late and we must prepare this group of stayovers for the evening at the Cathedral. The night-time noises and spirits can be sometimes overpowering. Those who have gone before you would remind us of the awful bombing during the War. This Cathedral was often used as a bomb shelter overnight because of its huge slabs of stone masonry.

"You can imagine the terrifying sounds for those taking shelter here especially at night. Shrieking streaming of bombardments as dense convoys of planes discharging their heavy loads of explosives; lighting up the night skies. A searing of memories lasting forever. A true Gothic horror story. A scary phantasmagoria."

Dietrick's days were unfolding into a dreamy uncertainty between past, present and future. His fantasy trips were more and more compelling for him to redirect his thinking away from his American thought world and into his German past, not before much clear dreams with his conscious mind. His subconsciousness was coming more and more to the fore.

"It appears," reasoned the rector, becoming more like a Father Confessor, "that you, Dietrick, are developing a split personality, a form of schizophrenia."

"What does this mean?" asked Dietrick.

"It means that your German-American background has been so conflicted and complicated by the traumas of the War."

"What about my roots in America?"

"Too early to tell yet with any precision. The pieces of the puzzle are incomplete and mixed up at this point. What do you now recall of your family in America?"

"Not much anymore, if I ever did."

"How sure are you of your American birth?"

"Not exactly."

"Could you have instead been born in Germany or an adjacent country?"

"Farfetched, but who knows at this point?"

"You still seem hazy about your name, Dietrick Knoblock."

"So, what's going on?"

"You were severely traumatized by the aerial bombardments over Cologne in World War II. Your infamy was no doubt here. And was reactivated in subconscious thought by the time spent now in the Cathedral. No doubt your parents took refuge here at night during the terrible bombing."

"Actually, I have long heard about the terrible toll taken by the people who were trying to stop the bombing but who were angry at the Allies for their attacks."

"Yours is an extra case of trauma's effects, but we have seen others like it here."

IV

The Deacon of Cologne Cathedral had a slightly different take on the whole matter to which he had been privy. "It sounds to me like a clinical case of amnesia brought about by the trauma of the War years here.

"Though transparency can occur in such cases where the traumatized part of the memory is transformed into another part of the conscious self and a juxtaposition of reality and unreality gets all jumbled together, leaving the patient seemingly rational but in fact hallucinatory."

"What does this mean in actual everyday terms?" asked the rector.

"It means that Dietrick could have blocked out of memory his actual German childhood background by transferring it to a partly imaginary American counterpart that may or may not be rooted in some form of reality."

"The question is how can we know for sure?" asked the rector.

"Let's ask him some questions. He obviously needs help."

"Dietrick, tell us more about your younger years in America, like where you come from. Are your parents still alive?"

"Thank you for your interest. I come from a city much like Cologne, with a big river and cathedral."

"What is its name?"

"Colony."

"Are your parents till there?"

"I think so."

"But you are not sure?"

"No."

"Why do you scream out here at night about bombs dropping?"

"I'm not aware of that."

"How, as an American, do you speak or yell with a German accent on occasion?"

"Not sure."

"Do you ever feel that your family has secrets you do not want to share with others?"

"Maybe."

"When was the last time you spoke with any member of your family?"

"I can't remember."

"Would you like for us to contact your family for you?"

"No."

"Why not?"

"Too many problems."

"Do you feel at home or lost here in Cologne, or Germany as a whole?"

"I imagine."

"Where have you been all this time before coming to Cologne?"

"Wandering and being taken in."

"So, do you feel lost?"

"Lost?"

"What shall we do?"

"I don't know."

The questions came back once again to Dietrick Knoblock's name.

"How should we account for the same name you have from your apparent American past with the hero here in Germany during the War?"

"A good question," responded Dietrick to the deacon and rector, all three by now cooperating with each other in their eagerness to get to the bottom, even if Dietrick continued to exhibit signs of bizarre and erratic behavior.

But still, no real answers or solutions. What to do?

V

The International Red Cross, with its strong American influence, had a big part to play in the post-war reordering of Germany and other West European countries. Among these efforts were the caring for the injured and those with family traumas. The widespread devastation was brought about on both sides, far away on the German border with buzz bombs sent over London from there but resulting in Allied bombings of Rotterdam.

The issue of misplaced persons and the like was an enormous problem, affecting both sides in the War's aftermath. By the time we are dealing with here, the throngs of people in Europe who were misplaced by War had persisted after the War' immediate aftermath.

The longstanding bombed-out result of the Cathedral was testament to the devastation and surrounding human suffering long afterward.

The International Red Cross, led by America, took over much of the case of Dietrick Knoblock, as best it could. This meant that the US side of his life's story would now become center focus, more so than with the Cathedral officials.

"Before we can proceed further in this case," explained the US Red Cross field person, "we need to establish what the exact limited database is that we have for displaced persons in the US as a result mostly of the War in Europe.

"There is no such name as Dietrick Knoblock in the database that correspondents with any actual known identity that we have been able to investigate in the US, much like Europe," according to another case worker back in Germany.

Meanwhile, what to do with the purported Dietrick Knoblock? Few or none of his own clues seemed, so far, to have panned out or led very far. Where was he? In fact, he had shipped unknowingly—on his own—back to the US via Red Cross, to continue his sightseeing there, somewhat oblivious of his condition and surroundings, but apparently able to get around. Fortunately for his own wellbeing, he was found and temporarily institutionalized.

VI

When our Dietrick (reverting to his former name) met up, by circumstance, with Sallie at the American Red Cross Sanitorium, where he had been detained, she was being discharged from her own stay there. He managed somehow to slip past the authorities there to join her on her car ride to Duluth, Minnesota, where she would be resuming her former checkered way of life, living off government subsidies, somewhat like Dietrick himself with his various aliases as well as his confused state of mind.

"Tell me about Duluth," he asked Sallie (assuming that was her real name too).

"It's a small port city on Lake Superior."

"Near the Mississippi River?"

"Somewhat."

"Sounds a little like a city I was at on the Rhine River."

"Don't know about that. I was never there."

"What's Duluth like?"

"Okay, but people interfere often in each other's business. It can drive each other crazy."

"I know what you mean."

"This traveling on the Interstate highway can tire one out after a while," said Sallie.

"There's a rest stop up ahead. Let's pull over and get something to eat and get some sleep here in the car."

"Okay."

"Do you ever have sex with strangers?" asked Dietrick.

"I need to have a good orgasm at least once a week."

"Me too. How do you do it usually, Sallie?"

"It does not matter. Whatever does the trick."

"Like what?"

"It has been hard to find a regular way, so I do it myself or with another female, like with the young woman I would masturbate with in the Red Cross sanitorium, but she became very jealous and threatened to harm me if I did it with anyone else."

"Would you want to do it with me?" asked Dietrick.

"Not intercourse. I don't use birth control and wouldn't want to get pregnant again. One abortion is enough. Condoms don't satisfy me enough."

"Agreed."

"Anyway, guys aren't as good as another woman to be able to massage my clitoris into a good orgasm."

"Unless I am able to give you good oral sex?"

"Maybe."

"You want to try?"

"Let's double over on this front seat and try oral sex first. Take off your pants and skirt."

"STOP! EVERYBODY OUT! THIS IS INTERSTATE POLICE!"

The police car's red lights flashing. The couple and their car were written up in the police records and eventually permitted to travel on. Evidently, this was a favorite spot for such kinds of interactions.

By the time, two or more days later, the pair finally reached Duluth, events were unfolding more dramatically. With the police car's records becoming available to such sensitive places as the Red Cross Sanitorium, which was already trying to track down where Dietrick and Sallie had gone, someone as lethal as Sallie's female lover at the sanitorium could pose a problem for those concerned, along with Dietrick's unbalanced and unpredictable state of mind.

VII

When the authorities involved eventually tracked down and arrived at Sallie's place of residence in Duluth, Minnesota, they found the small lakeside community in great consternation. There had been a bloody murder with no apparent motive. The victim was Sallie, the focus of hate had been her crotch, now ripped apart by some kind of butcher knife—sorry to report the terrible details. Obviously, the revenge of a psychopath, bent on making a public statement. But who?

Detrick was nowhere to be found, there or elsewhere, despite their many recent sightings together over extensive areas.

How might Sallie's female lover play a part? She, herself had also been discharged by the Sanitorium and was no longer to be located.

"A real question," construed the legal investigator in the case, Sergeant Gilbert, "is whether another woman could have committed such a heinous, barbaric murder. It's hard to imagine Sallie's female lover could have done such a thing."

"Yes," said his assistant, Detective Swift, a woman herself, "but as the old saying goes, hell hath no fury like a woman scorned. Anyway, so far, she seems to be the only one who would have a motive."

Added her partner: "We must investigate the situation at the Sanitorium as well as with anyone having similar problems here in Duluth. First of all is the whereabouts of Dietrick Knoblock, or whatever is his name."

VIII

At this point, Dietrick was long gone to different parts, still in a vague sort of state of mind, sometimes without exactly knowing it.

He was continuing his search for his identity, name, home, and purpose, but apparently with little or no cognizance of the murder and investigations back in Duluth, Minnesota, now left behind. He was more intent now as before on seeing new sights, of which there were plenty in the Great Lakes regions.

What next?

With asylum guardians in pursuit, Dietrick possibly a danger to others or himself, he made his way across the Great Lakes into Canada. Being a suspect in the grisly murder of Sallie, he managed to elude, almost without realizing it, the authorities trying to locate him, especially in connection with the terrible murder. Sometime thereafter, ever on the move in a restless state of mind, he was able to get passage, freighter bound, for the UK. Arriving back in the UK and on to Germany—where he had started from— he was more disoriented than before.

IX

"It's almost inevitable," exclaimed Detective Swift to her partner in the Minnesota mystery murder case.

"I know what you mean," he replied. "It's as if the system by itself brought back that guy for justice."

They were referring to Interpol, the international criminal organization based in Lyons, France, comprising nearly 200 nations. Interpol had at last tracked down Dietrick but under a different name shown to be no more verifiable than his other aliases over time, and he was a proverbial 'space cadet'.

The Interpol coordinator in this case, Ms. Judson, centered in the US, suspected from the start that some unusual facts of the murder itself pointed in some disturbing directions. She and the Minnesota detective, Swift, together soon took their cases directly to the Sanitorium, where Dietrick and the murder victim had been last seen together.

"By now, the more serious term, asylum, would be more applicable here due to the criminality involved."

Ms. Judson went on, "Has anyone found a reason for the unusual manner of the murder?"

"You mean the horrible slashing of the pelvic areas?" asked Swift. "Yes. Does that give any clues beyond just letting the victim bleed to death?"

"Yes," replied the female director of the asylum where Dietrick and Sallie had stayed. "Sallie was well known here for her extreme views on abortion rights but Dietrick did not exhibit any extreme views. Whoever committed this murder was criminally insane, which is not what Dietrick or Sallie were."

X

"Welcome back once again, Dietrick, to your old haunts here at bomb-stricken Cologne Cathedral," exclaimed the same rector as before. "By now, your life path must seem like an ever rotating pinwheel, with a constantly revolving uncertainty."

"You're right," responded Dietrick. "The same police chief as last time noted that very same sentiment too."

"The same Deacon as before has been expecting your return after reading the report about you through the International Red Cross and Interpol. He feels you may need our help here more than ever before."

"Yes. Thank you. I should tell you that on my way back here on an arc up around Northern America and Europe, I stopped for a while in England to see as well the ruins of the Nazis. Rocket attacks over London, now still showing wreckage so soon after the War."

"I'm sure that disturbed you too."

"Indeed. Horrible wreckage from the Nazi buzz bombs over the London Big Ben areas."

"What else?"

"I learned that the German rockets were constructed in part by some of my own Knoblock family members, a long hidden secret because of their memberships in the Nazi party. I have long suspected something like that and perhaps something worse."

"Do you feel that this family secret hurts you and your family honor?"

"Of course."

"How about the suffering London citizens who lived through those terrible aerial attacks?"

"Every night I relive in my waking and sleeping dreams those events, like viewing some kind of Gothic horror theater with vivid wall-flashing lantern lighting projected across the wall, sometimes with my screams wildly out loud."

"What about inside Germany during the War?"

"I've also learned from post-war reports inside England that among those apparent heroes at that bridge near Cologne on the Rhine that one of the pro-Nazi individuals trying to blow it up to stall an Allied advance inside Germany was named Knoblock. A terrible shock."

"How so?"

"It all seems to add up to a huge psychological complex of personalities."

"It's good to see you coming to such insights and conclusions by yourself, without my leading the witness, as the saying goes."

XI

Interpol's Judson caught up again with Dietrich Knoblock in Cologne over the issues involving the murder of Sallie back in Duluth.

"We have reason to believe that you could be a danger to yourself and to others, and that we need to incarcerate you in a secure facility either here in Germany or back in the US."

"Why?" asked Dietrich.

"There is still outstanding the unsolved murder of your friend Sallie in Duluth. You remain a prime suspect."

"I have no recollection of any of that."

"That in itself is part of your problem. The rector and deacon here at the Cathedral have concluded. You are suffering from extreme forms of psychosis that impairs your sense of reality This renders your potential for violence, even murder, a distinct possibility."

"Tell us more about these voices you hear usually at night with scary images of Gothic horror scenes," asked the rector in the presence of the little group.

"It's like we've already said, a split personality or multiple personalities. Sometimes I don't know the real me or another set of mes. It may go back," Dietrich further said, "to traumas I suffered as a child, especially the bombardments during the War, or the guilt I still feel from ties to the Nazi past we all have renounced in the past."

"So where does that leave us now?" asked the rector.

"It leaves us in a difficult situation," reasoned Interpol's Judson. "Because of the different states of consciousness involved, including separate individuals, it becomes hard to know who is doing what to whom at any given time, whether by the conscious or unconscious selves, separately or together. Guilt and innocence become harder to determine."

"But I keep reminding you all that I was not Sallie's killer, but rather someone else with extreme views on abortion rights or right to life. Very different from Sallie's," protested Dietrick.

"Maybe so," replied Judson.

At this unfortunate point, Dietrich Knoblock was killed one night by a falling block of stone dislodged from the Cathedral ceiling as he walked around in darkest evening all alone, without protective gear in a still dangerous reconstructive period in the badly damaged structure. So badly damaged was his psyche and memory that his early identity, birthplace, and family background, and the like could not be further determined with any further clarity. (Nor could much else be gleaned about the murder of Sallie, who herself was already, of course, along with the few other suspects in the crime.)

An elusive Gothic ghost story of its own latter-day kind with phantom-like actors or a phantasmagoria without end.

Part Four

Painterly Fantasies in Short Dreams

1. Oscar's Hollywood Crackup

Oscar grew up near Hollywood Hills in Southern California. Nothing luxurious but modestly comfortable; plenty of exposure to the nearby film industry. His friends thought him too star-struck by all the local luminaries, but his parents dismissed this as something he would grow out of. Instead, an obsession with the glitterati of the nearby film world took over his imagination, until all sorts of implausible scenarios came to cloud his sense of reality, noticeably so to others.

For Oscar, this pinnacle of fame circled around F. Scott Fitzgerald's presence there as a screen writer on various motion pictures starring notable actors and actresses; often behind the scenes as much as up front; imagine Oscar's day when through circumstances he actually came across the great writer Fitzgerald himself, who sensed in the fledging younger enthusiast a spirit reminiscent of his own younger years.

In time, the two found occasions to share with each other some of their Hollywood and other experiences, including their feelings of being an outsider with no other real feeling of belonging to something greater than themselves but still seeking a higher recognition for themselves. Each had his own somewhat troubled private life, Fitzgerald's, of course, we much better know.

"Tell me," began Fitzgerald on one occasion, "how did you get the name Oscar, a family name or just made up by your parents?"

Pausing for a moment as if hesitant to answer the question. "Actually neither, but given by myself as a nickname."

"Curious, any connection with the Academy Awards called the Oscars?"

"Well, yes."

"How so?"

"I never liked the strange name my parents gave me as a Junior to my father as Senior. This caused friction when I was growing up, and the kids at school made fun of me and mispronounced it."

"That's it?"

"There's more. I have long longed for achievement and recognition as a screenwriter like you."

"And you figure winning the Oscar for screenwriting is the ultimate achievement?"

"Yes."

"I can tell you that winning an Oscar would not solve all your problems, and I suspect there's more than that troubling you, Oscar. I myself never won an Oscar for anything. I and my wife Zelda have suffered from alcoholism and mental depression on and off for many years."

"But you have literary fame?"

"Not all, it seems. A book is being prepared called *The Crackup*, which tells of a terrible predicament. Don't go down that road."

Eventually, problems arose in this improbable relationship.

Oscar became a troubled hanger-on hoping for the master's literary fame by borrowed light. For his part, F. Scott saw the younger writer deluded (?) like wife Zelda's crackups landing her in an asylum.

"What have you done?" asked the great one. "Have you been stealing my materials for use under your own name?"

"Not at all," came the unconvincing reply.

"You're doing exactly what my third-rate novelist of a wife Zelda is trying to do to me. First it was my novels she was copying, now my film scripts."

Over time, the unacknowledged borrowings by Oscar became so entangled with Scott's own compositions that the disentanglement by editors and lawyers became very difficult down to more recent times.

"Oscar, you're talking in your own sleep. Your obsession with Academy Awards and literary fame is getting the better of you."

And there the story ends. Story and dream end.

2. The Happy Hookeress

In literature, as in art, fiction and artifice can be more real or compelling than the actuality being portrayed or accounted for. Take, for instance, Madame Defarge in Dicken's *Tale of Two Cities*. There she sat, with guillotine looming, while knitting the names of those to be executed in the Reign of Terror during the French Revolution. The novel's portrait has often been taken as the real deal.

Let's ask Madame Defarge exactly what or how she is knitting.

"What kind of knitting is it?"

"It's called Hookeress, a thick knit, a form of crochet. I sit here day after day by the platform seeking revenge against wicked people as their heads are getting chopped off in such an awful public spectacle."

"It gives you plenty of room to indicate names and deeds of those to be put to death."

"Yes."

"It keeps you plenty busy as you sit here each day."

"Of course."

"I suppose all this explains why you call it a Happy Hookeress because of the good vibes the stitching gives as each person's name is knitted and their head is being severed from their body in final justified agony."

"You're so right."

"What else?"

"These wicked aristocrats are sex perverts as well. So the women are, in effect, harlots and hookers, with hookeress impulses. All this again makes them so happy."

"This reminds me, looking ahead in time, to the book and movie in the 1970s called *The Happy Hooker* by and about Xaviera Hollander, as a professional call girl."

"How so?"

"It's made up of her circles arranged in broad patterns in various colors. The stitching itself is the main thing."

3. British Sweetness and Light

The celebrated late Victorian British writer, Matthew Arnold, might well have praised much later in time the civilizing force of cultural 'Sweetness and light' (his famous term) upon American as well as British thinking at the royal wedding of an heir of the throne to a half Afro-American Hollywood star.

"What a beautiful celebration of a mixed marriage, sure to reverberate far ahead in times to come," as Matthew Arnold could well have put it.

Said Queen Elizabeth II at the wedding reception, it could be imagined, "My two predecessors, Queens Victoria and Elizabeth I, are much present here today in spirit if not also in body." The sermon preached at the service stressed the power of love, with many scriptural citations.

Added Queen Victoria, "Don't forget the reference to Peter II about a thousand years being as if one day and a thousand days in the presence of the Lord."

"Time is fleeting and relative," exclaimed Elizabeth I, from back in centuries past.

Another scripture said "that with God, all things are possible", to the effect all sorts of multidimensional frame works can be entertained in the here and now.

"I readily agree with all this, but always remember that without culture, there tends to be anarchy. Culture of the right kind affords us all an enhanced civilization and sweetens what might become bitter fruits," as Matthew Arnold added.

4. Life is but a Dream, Sweetheart

A popular romantic song from the 1950s was called *Life is but a Dream, Sweetheart*. It was filled with special meaning for Harriet and Roger. For they had come of age as teenagers ready for romance in the midwestern town and high school that had become so familiar and comfortable to them. Imagine their discomfort when, at the end of their senior year, their families relocated far away from each other and they saw each other no more, without any further contact between the two youngsters in distant eras long before future forms of modern telecommunications. Over time, in later years, their separate lives grown far apart, without so much as glimpses at high school reunions or secondhand sightings through home grown.

And yet, the echo of that popular song sung by Perry Como so long ago stayed with Harriet and Roger. *Life is but a Dream, Sweetheart.*

Eons ahead in their 'golden years', as each was almost 80, still recalling their love for 'the oldies' in popular songs long gone to changing pop culture, the lure of that hit tune had not faded.

Then one night, out of a deep sleep, Harriet called out the name, "Roger, where are you?" Her husband had long been deceased. Getting out of bed, Harriet went to her mechanical devices and turned on YouTube to hear, for the first time, that old song by Perry Como. Having been by her now deceased husband in the electronic age, Harriet was even fascinated by the possibilities of mental telepathy. "Dreaming too," she told a friend, "has a special power."

Actually, hearing Perry Como singing about life as a dream brought back long ago feelings for Roger and their youth. Several days later, a man appeared at Harriet's residence wondering about her. He was a writer operating under his writer's name, Stuart. Through the web on his iPhone, Stuart had tracked Harriet down to her much later residence, which, as fate would have it, was still fairly close by. There they stood on her porch, as if quizzing each other in disbelief about their true identities, for each to the other seemed too different by now. His wife was deceased, and so resumed the beginnings of their renewed feelings for each other.

"But there are still too many loose ends here," said Harriet to Roger, "too many dream-like fantasies mixed with reality."

"Like what, us together?"

"Like how come you came to my door after all these decades at precisely the same time after my dream fantasies about you and us so long ago when we were teenagers?"

"Can sleeping thought-waves radiate out like?"

Ever the pop-scientist he was back in his youth, Roger asked out loud, "Do thought-waves really exist?"

"I've been hearing more and more in the news about 'artificial intelligence'."

"Yes, me too," responded Roger. "And don't forget Freud's famous early works on the nature and power of dreams in paranormal psychology."

"The power itself can often transcend human psychology."

"And leave things hanging in the balance?"

5. Till the End of Time, Mrs. Robinson

Another popular romantic song from the 1950s was *Till the end of Time*. It too sparked vivid memories of its era long after it first appeared. Still another favorite echoing down through the ages for guys and girls coming of age in the late 1960s was *Here's to you, Mrs. Robinson*, from the movie *The Graduate*.

The physics teacher was using simple analogies his high school students would readily understand and identify with.

"So time," she said, "is a relative concept as Einstein showed varying conditions with changing frameworks."

"I still don't understand," spoke up a student.

"Try this," said the teacher. "Einstein once said that touching a hot stove for a minute would seem to last an hour, but sitting next to a pretty girl for an hour would seem to last for a minute."

So the songs from the 50s and 60s, which you cite, could seem to reverberate forever, whereas a boring physics problem might be passed quickly out of mind?

"I suppose so."

(Laughter)

"Mrs. Robinson's seduction of the young man, Benjamin, in the movie, *The Graduate*, is a timeless tale," the teacher went on. "In a sense, there is no beginning or end. Just so infinity without start or finish."

"Now I see," voiced another student. "The so-called Big Bang that started the universe in the first place could not have occurred because there was no material condition originally beforehand to give rise for the bang."

"So there was no big bang?"

Laughter.

"Not if all is only spirit and not material, unless there are other kinds of universes we don't know about yet or never will."

At the end of the class, one male student was heard saying to another, "That is one dicey broad, for a physics teacher."

Agreed another male student, "I think she likes us, a real Mrs. Robinson. A timeless Mrs. Robinson?"

6. Riding the LGBTQ Lines

He wanted to remain nameless for the time being in order to protect himself from any adverse publicity getting back to his small close-knit hometown. There everybody knew him and his extended family as normal and upright so his intention was to carry forth their good honorable name.

Our subject felt the need to explore the outside world now that he was outside the family nest and independent from parents, yet still living at home; not far from the nearby major big city and metropolitan center where he often went to visit and hang out.

Trying to become familiar with the big city and complex subway system, our subject was especially puzzled by the trains marked 'LGBTQ Lines'. "What is that all about?" he asked someone.

"That's for riders who want to explore their sexuality," came the reply.

"How does that work?"

"First, you have to know what the letters stand for."

"Okay, tell me."

"Well, L is for Lesbian, G is for Gay, B is for Bisexual, T is for Transgender, and Q is for Questioning or Queer, plus a few others. All in the Oxford Dictionary."

"Then what?"

"Then you ride those lines, depending on what your preferences are—just one or two, or I suppose all somehow together."

"What's the purpose?"

"To meet up and get together with those you most identify with."

"Not straight?"

"Then you're not riding the LGBTQ lines, but something else."

"Should I give it a try?"

"Go ahead. Just slide your metro card in the turnstile and take your pick of which lines to go on. Each line has the usual station stops, so you can get on or off and transfer."

By the time our subject, Lenny, had tried and done all this a number of times, he had traveled the LGBTQ lines extensively. But how do we now know him by his real name Lenny? Guess what? There was no longer any need to fear bad hometown publicity for him when traveling the LGBTQ lines.

For, on every line, there were dozens of his hometown fellow citizens who knew him by name and called out his name with greetings such as, "Hi Lenny, good to see you."

Where had they all been hiding for so long?

7. Born to be Vile

"It's true," exasperated the property manager.

"It must be in her genes," affirmed her associate manager.

Their supervisor was all ears, for she too had seen for herself. Even the owner of their apartment rental company as well as the local precinct had had many run-ins with Jessica, who usually managed to stay one step ahead of everybody, obviously manipulating the rental codes and agencies to avoid being evicted or even jailed for her vile behavior. Complicating the plot were Jessica's few friends and relatives who were in and out of her sordid affairs, as if to reinforce the notion of things being somehow in her genes.

So what to do? Nothing so far had worked. Further interplay of ideas developed among parties involved. The point had come to hire an outside contractor.

"What does that mean?"

"But don't ask."

"But who will take care of things?"

"John."

"Who is he; a local contractor?"

"You got it."

"Is that some sort of pun?"

"He has a restaurant on Mulberry Street."

"Oh my god, you don't mean…?"

(Silence) Things were already getting hazy enough without further to do.

"Up a short way from the restaurant on Mulberry Street is the back side of Old St. Patrick's Cathedral. It's still an active place of worship for the locals down there, especially Italians."

"So how does all this tie in with things?"

Sometime after the proceeding occurrences and conversations, it so happened that our dear Jessica had arranged to have dinner with a timely acquaintance named Raoul to explore ways to eliminate her problem-people trying to get her evicted from her undervalued luxury apartment so the landlord could get new tenants paying much more rent, thereby getting rid of two birds with one stone—her vileness and low rent.

It turned out that, oddly as can happen through strange coincidences, this same Raoul under a different name was the same person Jessica was setting up to do her own dirty work. Hence, two middlemen in one, each one keeping the other guessing? Or a double switch? But who might be on whose side? Each side, landlord and tenant, felt they were finding the right middleman or point man. Sounds like an improbable double cross? But wait—whose side are you betting on?

Clever guy Raoul was, of course, looking out for himself, playing both sides against the other.

Here was where the restaurant and cathedral came together on Mulberry Street, in lower Manhattan.

On the same day, security was arranged by Raoul for each side to perform a hit on the other side; it was set for the tenant's guy to do the job at the restaurant, the tenant's guy was ready to do the hit at the cathedral down in the 'tomb' in the basement, where a guard was usually stationed at the entrance. But on the designated day, the guard was out sick with no one else to cover. So Jessica's demise was foiled; therefore, the celebration by the landlord had to be postponed. Later on, both sides had feelings of victory and defeat. But overall, everything seemed to be back to square one, with Jessica born to be vile and maybe snatching victory from the jaws of defeat as well as defeat from the jaws of victory?

8. The Big Business Wars

"It seemed in those days that everyone wanted to come to Madison Avenue to make their mark in the big advertising agencies. The dominating image of David Ogilvy, looking ever so tweedy and successful, was a definite drawing card for college grads starting out in the business world in the early 1960s when I too was doing the same."

So reminisced Otto Gierke many decades later when human diversity was more apparent and people like him felt less like outsiders. "The diversities in the universities whence come today's grads is wondrous." Otto somewhat felt flippantly yet approvingly: "So people like me stand a better chance being not so preppy."

But Otto had long since gone on to other kinds of ad agencies where he found, to his dismay, a less civilized, more brutal, even dog-eat-dog, atmosphere, which he dubbed 'the big business wars'.

His own particular problem was not so much the wars between companies but the internal struggle within companies.

"Your imagination is getting the better of you," said Otto's wife, Ankela, after a night of bad dreams for him.

"How so?"

"You kept calling out in your sleep for a rescue from bad business competitors seeking to have your body dumped into our local river."

Strangely enough, Otto was found a week later clinging to life in a local hospital after being thrown into the river under very bad circumstances.

"What do you remember?" asked his wife at his hospital bedside.

"Not much except for two people calling me an intellectual property thief over some business accounts from others inside my agency."

"Was all that in your imagination or real?"

"I don't know."

A hospital doctor, listening, said, "The power of mental suggestion is sometimes a fantasy state in which the patient suffers from amnesia and acts out the fantasy, sometimes with dangerous consequences."

But there was much more to come. In an unexpected twist in the story, Otto eventually, and with his wife's encouragement, soon gave up on the big business wars and devoted his time to writing fiction stories featuring large doses of fantasy trips with all sorts of borderline craziness that drew a goodly audience. Many are the ways in which writers come to their true calling; however, sometimes convoluted through arduous self-discovery.

9. A Day at the Office

This was 'bring your child to the office day', an annual event at our office. It was meant to be a pleasant 'getting to know you' occasion. It quickly turned out to be anything but.

"It seemed like the beginning of a perfect day," said Marjorie to husband Jake after they had both come home from work, he from a computer company and she from a utility business, where for both orderliness was de rigueur, something both parents were trying to instill in the kids, who tended to be rowdy.

"Were there problems with Tina and Toby (ages 12 and 10) at your office?"

"Not exactly," responded Marjorie.

"So what then?"

"The people at Mom's office behave like schoolyard nut jobs," piped up Tina with her usual impetuosity.

"Seconded," Toby said. "Today, Tina and I were the well-behaved ones and the office staff the crazies."

"Today, at least, it was all true, an unexpected turn of events," lamented Marjorie to Jake.

"What happened?"

"My supervisor, Tillie, came to work after a long weekend of heavy drinking with her boyfriend. She acted still lopped in the office this morning. She pushed the wrong button for the elevator and the fire alarm went off, bringing fire trucks and pandemonium. So the company's president sent her home at lunch time to sober up, leaving me to fill in even though I had no experience like Tillie had at that level.

"Then a shouting match erupted with different factions in the departments. I was left to manage as best I could in the afternoon, an important meeting, with me unprepared. The kids thought it must be the end of the world somehow, and frankly, so did I."

"But our mom got through it all, didn't you, Mom?"

"Thanks to you two there with me to help me keep my sanity."

"An interesting reversal of roles for children's day at the office," concluded Jake.

10. The Deserted Shop

A deserted house is one thing, where successions of family dwellers might be expected to conjure deep and lasting memories almost as ghosts living forth their own kinds of reality.

But a deserted shop? Especially in the middle of nowhere as this one was, with no real succession of personal owners and scheduled for demolition?

Don't say that to the young man who had lost possessions or his shop after only a few years there and now found himself wandering about through the vacated structure and remembering all the wonderful transactions there.

Our young man was indulging in his own 'meditations on ventures past'. Yes, spirits were speaking to him. No, you don't believe in ghosts? Don't say that to famous authors past like Henry James, for whom ghosts were real and tangible, not just some form of medically induced hallucinations, such as with morphine.

"Who or where am I?" puzzled our young man, not yet fully conscious of his name after slowly awakening from a dreamlike state. He was dozing in and out of alertness in a hospital bed with two doctors and a relative looking on. His name was not yet assigned, which he knew enough must be odd. It was all surreal.

"Never mind," answered one of the doctors, reassuring but firm.

"What happened to my deserted shop that I was visiting?"

"Don't worry," said the relative. "They are treating you here with an altered state of mind and body, with your previous permission."

"This is an ongoing experimental procedure to see if it helps you communicate with those no longer living who were prior beings connected to your shop."

"Do you now recognize your deceased relative standing here?"

"I think so. She's the one who got me the shop in the first place."

"Correct. You can see her here but not talk to her, at least not yet."

"So what's going on that you can tell me about?"

"We here are in an experimental program exploring new dimensions of artificial intelligence, going far beyond mere robots."

Our young man is regaining awareness of the assembled group.

"Could that someday mean that ghosts will actually be real, not just in fantasy dreams?"

"Yes."

"Or that such a phenomenon will in the distant future and become a key part of intergalactic travel in search of other advanced beings?"

"Yes."

So our young man had become part of a scientific break-
through, with more to come.

11. Brahim and Sherifa

"When the authorities, slow to act, finally came to their small apartment, they naturally found the grief-stricken couple upset that it had taken so long…"

Thus began the local news account of the crime and aftermath. Somehow, many townspeople back then had a premonition of bad things to come for these new strangers coming to live in their midst. Brahim and Sherifa and their several children were all dressed and acting as the devout peace-loving Muslims from the Middle East where they had emigrated from to America.

"The mysterious, yet uninvestigated murder of their eldest son, Atmi, was something no one seemed to want to handle," experts for the newspaper reported. "They have been feared by some as outsiders in this town, unaccustomed to their ways. Living peacefully in our midst, though perhaps too close for many people's comfort, the Muslim family had seemed to adjust to the American way of life. Brahim had been a part-time superintendent of a small walk-up apartment building, working other night jobs to provide for his family. Sherifa was working for a company, cleaning offices, while the kids were attending the local public school."

"So who," asked the police sergeant rather rhetorically, "could have committed this murder?"

"Hard to tell at this point," shrugged the precinct captain. "A lot of nut jobs out there."

The couple's jobs now seemed in jeopardy.

"Too dangerous to handle anymore," noted one of their bosses.

"How do we handle the kids?" asked a school principal.

"But back to the basic questions about the murder," asked the local newspaper.

Then things began to accelerate. Suspicion began to point to a tenant in Brahim's building, as a possible perpetrator of a hate crime. The police came under criticism for being too lax against hate crimes, especially if it was with their own prejudices toward 'strange' immigrants. And the 'liberal' news people provoked criticism for their own biases.

"In the end," reported the local newspaper, "the crime was solved. And things returned to normal, with few lessons learned, unfortunately."

12. Countdown

"The jobs of a military leader, technological overseer, and political coordinator are today becoming more and more interdependent in times of potential nuclear war." The President was clearly worried as he sat at his desk in the Oval Office, talking to several close aides. "At any given moment in an emergency, we need to be ready to pull everything together and act in the right way."

"And to be of one mind to get things done," added another aide, "as in the situation at hand."

"Let's suppose, as is sometimes said, that President Roosevelt knew, in advance, that the Japanese fleet was on its way to attack Pearl Harbor but let it happen to make congress and the people go to war. Would he act the same way today? Or would he be accused of treason or a crime?"

The President's aides were divided and uncertain as to what the President might be getting at.

"Or President Jefferson tried today to make a secret deal with Spain to make a deal to buy the Louisiana Purchase behind Congress' back…would he still get away with it?"

Again, the aides were divided and puzzled, sensing that something was up his sleeve.

"Or could Allied Commander Eisenhower have pulled out of the Normandy invasion absolute secrecy of the unfolding plans long before the event?"

Then came the zinger. "What would happen in this day and age, with all the military, technological, and political leverage by me, if I found it necessary to order a preemptive strike on another nation, shown at (trigger point?) to do the same to us, without any prior consultation by me or anyone else so as to achieve utmost secrecy for success?"

One aide: "It might set in motion a fateful countdown by each of the opposite sides."

"But what might be the consequences if I do not do this by a preemptive strike?"

"Possibly far worse consequences?"

"Could I still act like Roosevelt, Jefferson, or Eisenhower with impunity if motivated by the higher necessity of the national good?"

Something was clearly up but not yet clear, but soon it would become clear. For the countdown had already begun, but on which side? All this before anyone was informed about what to do now.

13. Murder in the Oval Office

"How plausible would it be for a murder to occur in the President's Oval Office, as the basis for a novel's plot?" asked Claud Pepper, thinking of writing one himself.

His editors for previous books thought it too implausible because of all the restrictions in place there today. "After all," said Sheila Cantor, "the Oval Office is where the president does most of his actual work and receives official visitors strictly blocked off even from the west wing of the larger White House."

"But so many novels have been written about murders of all kinds, including the West Wing and executive branch, not to mention the departments and agencies. Why not one on just the Oval Office by itself?"

"You would have to take accounting of all the special security in place there in this day and age. There are guards by the entrance doors. All sorts of electronic surveillance. The hidden buttons for the president to lock the doors in an emergency. Even the windows are prevented from producing vibrations that enemies could convert into voices revealing everything being said, as Russian agents were once able to achieve."

But Claude was still not deterred by Sheila's playing of the devil's advocate on such a novel's believability or even its repetition of similar DC murder mysteries by other novelists. So he managed to go see for himself by working his way through contacts into the pool of reporters covering the White House on a near daily basis.

A good shot at this, after all.

Claude eventually hit his mark, and then some. On one golden rare moment, he was briefly able to look into the Oval Office when the president himself, President Rathbone (or Bonehead as press people sometimes called him) was there in a receptive mood, talking casually with reporters there quite by chance. It so happened that Claude's recognition as a novelist on other topics was picked up on by no less than President Rathbone himself and, you guessed it, Claude was able to ask directly for the president's input on the murder mystery's plot or main idea.

"Good idea," said Rathbone. "Your editor is correct about believability with the Oval Office so well guarded. So make it some sort of cyber or electronic attack that incapacitates all those safeguards."

"Thank you, Mr. President," said Claude.

As he left, the president jokingly said, "Just don't have the novel's plot be about the murder of the president." Then he would try to gain direct insight into the Oval Office's workings whether the president was there or not there.

"Go for it," urged Shelia. "You might have something. But don't have a president called Mr. Bonehead."

So compelling became the president's own idea for the proposed novel by Claude Pepper and his literary editor, Sheila Cantor, that all three developed a working kind of collaboration to bring it to fruition. An unusual relationship was emerging behind the scenes. Things were starting off with Rathbone's proposed cyber attack on the Oval Office with a knockout blow to the safeguards already in place so as to enable some yet undecided strike on the president's life, all impossible if the safeguards were not first removed.

"This is indeed taking on a life of its own," said Claude, "but I still can't figure out how to set up a believable cyber attack on the Oval Office's safeguards."

"How about consulting a defense department specialist in cyber warfare?"

Sheila's suggestion, at first rejected, won out and was worked out but with dangers of ever widening circles.

"Yes," seconded a Pentagon spokesman, "not to comprise Pres. Rathbone in any of this."

"What we all must keep in mind are the limits, so far, of cyber capabilities but also the dangers of artificial intelligence and it's self-acting potential." This warning by another cyber expert in private industry might mean a bigger threat yet imagined to the Oval Office.

"Once set in motion through thought or action," wondered the president through a chief aide, "could misuse of artificial intelligence become irreversible once it's on?" Then machines take over.

"What could this mean for my story?" asked Claude. "Or has it grown way beyond me and the rest of us?"

In the midst of this extended back and forth over Claude Pepper's novel about murder in the Oval Office, hitting too close to real national security, a rare power outage has now occurred in the White House and Oval Office. Some reports suggest it's an inside job aimed at killing the President.

Thus, the overriding issue of the Daily Washingtonian, "The safeguards in the Oval Office have been compromised and penetrated, leaving the president himself vulnerable to deadly harm."

Things were now speeding up and the distinction between fantasy and reality becoming more and more blurred. Doubts were being raised on all sides. "Could a believable presidential murder actually be pulled off inside the confines and safeguards of the Oval Office itself?" That question was increasingly put to Claude Pepper by his editor, Sheila Cantor.

"The clincher has occurred in the affirmative for the President himself as a collaborator and a creator of the novel." That sentiment by the Pentagon's contact was agreeable to the novelist and editor.

"It involves a secret device in the Oval Office," he explained to the Pentagon contact, "that allows the president to turn off all electronic safeguards in the office when necessary in certain circumstances. But his momentary lapse, however secret, could allow a shrewd cyber enemy to take advantage and strike the president if the switch was not turned back on to safeguard him."

"But can electronic secret eyes and fingers always be counted on to do as directed?" asked the novelist and editor.

A few days later, the terrible news headline read, "President Rathbone found dead in Oval Office in chair, apparently a victim of electronic system switched off safeguards against attacks."

Everyone asked: "How could this happen?" "Was it some kind of twisted inside job?" "Or was it a futuristic double cross by a double agent?" "Or did the advanced artificial intelligence take over in some bizarre twist of fate?" "Did the (?) of the novel's (?) cast its own mysterious spell upon all involved?"

14. Trip to Mars

Desmond: "The candidates for a manned future flight to Mars are lining up. Why not me too?" As usual, with their son's overactive imagination, Archibald and Rosemary Hoyt, while not discouraging him, would typically humor him along in such a way as to have him see the improbability of it all.

"Be sure to have enough food and water for the long flight into outer space," Rosemary urged the teenager.

Added Archibald, "And also for the return flight."

This time, there was a new twist on Desmond's part. "I need Mother to come with me." He was serious, worrying his parents, who by now were seriously considering therapy for Desmond.

There had been other signs of an obsessive mother complex. Now, he wanted Mother all for himself into the vast forever of space and time.

"As a family therapist," began Dr. Freud in the first session, "I usually like to get some background information from the parents alone, then proceed to the children individually, then from there to the group as a whole."

Archibald brought up his own parents' great interest in the novelist Scott Fitzgerald's *Tender is the Night*, which included lots of Freudian psychology, especially concerning incest.

"My last name Hoyt figures in the novels involving a lot of themes about incest. My wife's married name, Rosemary Hoyt, seems to have been crucial to my choosing her as my wife, including my lust for her younger body. A kind of father-daughter incest impulse."

"I suppose," said Rosemary, "that our son, Desmond, feels competition with his father for my affection and attention; doesn't Freud talk about the Oedipus complex?"

"Yes, a theme going back to the ancient Greeks, where the son, Oedipus, seeks to kill his father and marry his mother. The reverse is the daughter's Electra complex and the daughter has sex with her father."

It eventually came in these kinds of conversations that Rosemary's father forcibly had intercourse with her when she was almost at puberty; moreover, Desmond, when he was very young used to put on his mother's clothes and masturbate when he was home alone.

At other sessions with Dr. Freud, Archibald pointed out that the plot and characters in *Tender is the Night* are vastly from the characters in Fitzgerald's other works. In the end, Fitzgerald believes, along with Freud, that such cases involving sexual and other types of traumas are never really resolved or ended, but remain in limbo.

In Desmond's mind, the question still went back to the mission to planet Mars at some future time. Since Mars's parents, Jupiter and Juno, were somewhat like Desmond's parents, because they exhibited a strong male figure and a yielding female form.

As of this writing, there are 41 persons named Rosemary Hoyt in the US public records office.

142

15. My Pad

Words of the same spelling can naturally sometimes get confused with each other, especially with people who are already prone to careless diction or slurred speech. This can lead to all sorts of miscommunication or even potential harm. In one case I know of, the result was a comedy of errors. In another, an error of comedies.

In the first case, a teenager named Lucy exclaimed to her boyfriend Mike, "I want to take off my pad, but don't throw it away." Mike thought this remark was odd, assuming Lucy was making a joke of needing to go to the bathroom at the movie theater to put on another sanitary napkin. In fact, Lucy was referring to the launch pad for a space rocket to take off from in the film they were watching. A kind of comedy of errors. What about Lucy later on finding out that Mike was making fun of her perceived irrational comments about her pad with his friends at school?

As if to put some sort of hex on Lucy's circle of girlfriends, Janet pulled a similar dimwitted use of language by asking George to come to 'my pad' after school, not meaning her house, but rather her sorority room.

Then there are the reverse kind of casts also likely to occur at 'comedy central' schools all over. There, 'my pad' could easily be used as a comic foil for 'my tool', except for the obvious lack of meaning.

And so it goes, stretching a point.

16. Who's Pinging Her Now?

An old popular love song by Connie Francis prompts a much different kind of variation on 'who's pinging her now?' Hers was a much simpler age where songs and sounds measured to the beats of more innocent impulses. Nowadays, the sexual suggestions fueling popular lyrics often seem to cloud over the native hues of good rhymes. The obvious sexual overtones of 'who's f---ing her now' would seem too vulgar in an age of anything goes, where conversations can be so easily misconstrued by whom and where can the lines be drawn. Does the same apply to our short story on 'My Pad'? Or even 'Trip to Mars'?

But let's not jump to conclusions. Actually, the 'pinging' in this story refers to the pinging or beeping sound produced by handheld cellphones when they are receiving incoming text messages, similar to the steadier ringing of landline phones. So is vulgarity often in the mind of the beholder? A relative standard varying between eras, places, and circumstances? How many 4-letter words, once shunned, become commonplace?

"I am constantly being pinged or beeped by incoming text messages on my iPhone," so a friend tells me, "especially since telemarketing has dramatically increased." Whenever I'm with her, the calls never cease coming in, day and night. It can drive one crazy.

"Some people I know have had really weird experiences," she went on one day. "One guy I knew was typically walking down on a wide city street when multiple pedestrians were walking intently with their heads down like robot phantoms, bumping into each other. Then one day my friend fell down an open doorway hatch on the sidewalk and had to be taken the hospital.

"There, oddly enough, on the way to the hospital, an EMS nurse started administering CPR, since she did not think he was breathing. He arose to the nurse's perceived kisses and touched her. Whereupon he asked her out on a date, but she spurned his advances."

So these stories of people using their iPhone or cellphone for messaging can be disruptive and confusing; not to mention annoying too, with all the incessant noises going on day and night.

One thing is certain for the faint of heart or easily offended: Who's pinging her now is not about some illicit nymphomaniac but realities of telecommunication and its absurdities.

17. Woman in the Fancy White Gown

There she stood. Picturesque. Perfect. The epitome of female beauty. Enough to suggest what such ideal dreams were made of. Surely this was not a reality. Or was it? Her white gown sparkled as if standing and meant for all to admire at a fancy dress ball. Her motionless pose was a statuesque attempt to attach a defining name to her. Classical statuesque beauty almost defying a description.

The picture gallery in the museum left little doubt for our nameless visiting couple strolling through the gallery to discover who the star attraction was.

Visitors were thronging to get up close to the woman in the fancy white gown to be able to catch a glimpse of her occasional famous wink and finger twitch teasing the museum-goers.

Again, there she stood, picture perfect and above all, that fancy white gown beyond compare.

Upon exiting the nearby park for lunch, our couple encountered a female mime standing on a pedestal for passers-by to admire and again to watch for signs of animation. There was none at this point. How could that be if the mime was clearly a human being and not an artificial construction? A human being could not remain frozen in posture for this long without signs of life such as the blinking of eyes.

The return to the gallery after lunch brought further consternation. The woman in the fancy white gown was now missing from her spot in the painting along with a few little alterations in her replacement in the group scene. No, it was not just a simple switch of canvases. This was confirmed by the museum staff who were themselves bewildered by the inexplicable change.

While all this was playing out, word was now circulating that the mime in the nearby park was now gone, vanished.

Where to find answers?

Enter Claude Monet himself, thus far curiously silent, at least in the ways we have been considering. Let's ask him directly about some of this. It so happens that in the same museum, there are a couple of self-portraits along with wider pictures of him.

"The painting of the woman in the fancy white gown is clearly meant to communicate qualities of ideal beauty with the viewer, transporting him beyond himself in a way from present physical beauty into a conscience almost too rare to describe or fathom."

"Is this what is partly meant by the viewer capturing the impression of the moment in time and space in a kind of artistic reality in which present dimensions of pure physicality are transcended and can sometimes be altered or even disappear?"

"In a way, yes. Each viewer can experience and translate for himself what that impression means."

"Does this help explain how the mime in the park or the woman in the white gown can play so-called tricks on our sense of reality?"

"You may well be right."

"It sounds like the artistic impression of a moment in space and time could lend itself to all kinds of illusionism depending on what the viewer sees."

"It depends on your own point of view."

"After this state of visual and physical reality or dreams, imaginations runs deep."

18. Next Time?

Endings have a way of becoming beginnings. Last times often lead to next times. Just when Dickens is preparing the reader for the finale of certain novels, another novel often opens up. Mozart actually teases the listeners of some of his symphonies into concluding that the last chords are done with, whole new ones are suddenly at hand, often with many pause endings to delight the listener. One might say that Claude Monet in his own way too was given to surprise continuous endings as his ethereal brushstrokes unfolded from canvas to canvas.

Over the course of this trilogy, the adventures of Claudette Monet have taken many new twists and turns as she ventured forth across Europe and America. Readers may recall a number of mysterious doings and surprise endings along the way.

Some of these were left open-ended, perhaps inviting readers to continue on the journey with Claudette and the others with her. It was a cacophony of occurrences. Where did it point to? Or was it too early to tell? A story of future, past, and present? We can't always tell.

Readers can imagine for themselves what all the people in the trilogy actually looked like. Can you reach out to them, or they to you?

www.ingramcontent.com/pod-product-compliance
Lightning Source LLC
Chambersburg PA
CBHW061526050726

47593CB00002B/686